I0591742

As Wide As I Can See

Mark Snyder

A SAMUEL FRENCH ACTING EDITION

SAMUEL FRENCH

FOUNDED 1830

SAMUELFRENCH.COM
SAMUELFRENCH-LONDON.CO.UK

FOR PRODUCTION ENQUIRIES

UNITED STATES AND CANADA
Info@SamuelFrench.com
1-866-598-8449

UNITED KINGDOM AND EUROPE
Plays@SamuelFrench-London.co.uk
020-7255-4302

Each title is subject to availability from Samuel French, depending upon country of performance. Please be aware that *AS WIDE AS I CAN SEE* may not be licensed by Samuel French in your territory. Professional and amateur producers should contact the nearest Samuel French office or licensing partner to verify availability.

MUSIC USE NOTE

IMPORTANT BILLING AND CREDIT REQUIREMENTS

AS WIDE AS I CAN SEE received its world premiere production in February 2012 by At Hand Theatre Company (Justin Scribner and Matt DiCarlo, producers) at HERE Arts Center in New York City. It was directed by Dan Horrigan; the scenic design was by David L. Arsenault; the costume design was by Nicole Wee; the lighting design was by Josh Bradford; the sound design was by Colin Whitely; casting was by Judy Bowman; graphic design was by Heather Weiss; photography was by Matthew Murphy; the production stage manager was Angela F. Kiessel; the assistant stage manager was Sophie Quist; and the production assistant was Laura Kim. The cast was as follows:

JESSICA	Julie Leedes
DEAN	Ryan Barry
TYLER	Joshua Levine
NAN	Kay Capasso
CHARLOTTE	Mèlisa Breiner-Sanders
WALT	Conan McCarty

Special Thanks: Hannah Bos, Chris Burns, Bethel Caram, Joshua Cole, Jessica Dey, Jessica Dickey, Jamie Effros, Ramsey Faragallah, Leeanne Hutchison, Chris Kipiniak, Nick Leavens, Mark Sullivan, William Austin Tidwell, and the Ohio Five.

CHARACTERS

JESSICA – 42, the head waitress at a popular local restaurant

DEAN – 30, a journalist/former news reporter living with Jessica

TYLER – 31, Dean's best friend, a mail carrier and stay-home father

NAN – 27, Tyler's girlfriend and the mother of his children

CHARLOTTE – 30, Dean and Tyler's visiting friend from high school

WALT – 48, Charlotte's husband

SETTING

Northeast Ohio

TIME

September, 2010

For my brothers,
Gregg Robert Snyder and Matthew Stephen Reese:
Always here, always home.

ACT ONE

Scene One

(The backyard of a small two-story house in a developing neighborhood of a small industrial city in northeastern Ohio, between Lake Erie and the Pennsylvania border. The house is aluminum-sided and we see the back/screen door with three steps down to a small cement patio. Lawn furniture is stacked against the side of the house, leading around to the driveway offstage. Perhaps a kitchen window adorned with a small flowerbox or herb garden is also in view.)

(Directly opposite the house on the other side of the stage is a small trailer home. The door and retractable steps down to the ground can be seen. Orange Halloween lights adorn the doorframe as well as a bumper sticker that reads BIG DICK.)

(The fence around the yard is clogged with debris around its edges – wet fallen leaves, mulch, and the errant wrappers thrown by kids passing by on the other side. One gets the feeling all of this has been continually raked into these corners over the years, to be dealt with later.)

(What there is to see of the actual yard is tiny; there is a tree stump in the back near the fence and a plastic wading pool set up. A hose runs from the other side of the house into the pool to keep it filled with water.)

(It is early afternoon on Sunday, during the Indian summer of fall, 2010.)

(JESSICA stands at the top of the concrete steps, as the screen door slams behind her. At the sound, DEAN emerges from underwater in the pool.)

DEAN. I hear you.

JESSICA. Ha.

DEAN. Both ears open –

JESSICA. – And plugged with water from that hose.

DEAN. I've got it all under control.

JESSICA. Get out of the kiddie pool, Dean.

DEAN. *Wading.*

JESSICA. You barely fit.

DEAN. Walmart calls it a wading pool, so it must be true. Walmart, babe.

JESSICA. Well, this "babe" is late for work.

DEAN. On a Sunday?

JESSICA. Training.

DEAN. Your name's practically engraved on the silverware in that joint.

JESSICA. Someone's got to show the new servers how to fold napkins and prep the salad dressing station. One's still got braces. Our break conversation should be a heap of fun.

DEAN. Why's that someone got to be you?

JESSICA. It's my shift to turn down.

DEAN. Today?

JESSICA. Pays time and a half.

DEAN. Fine.

JESSICA. I'm not asking your permission, Dean. You're gonna be on your own out here.

DEAN. So tell me –

JESSICA. *Again.*

DEAN. – Okay, *again* what to do. I'm listening.

JESSICA. Backstroking is what you're doing.

DEAN. Your dulcet tones would reach me if we were sitting off the coast of Maine.

JESSICA. Ooh la la. Now get out.

DEAN. Deep diving into the reefs of the Atlantic Ocean, surrounded by salmon and lobster, hovering over all with my trap in hand, catching the main course for our candlelit dinner –

JESSICA. "– At our homey little bed and breakfast."

DEAN. Whatever. We're going.

> (DEAN *sticks his trunked bottom in the air out of the pool.*)

JESSICA. You're always on vacation. Why do we need one together?

> (JESSICA *is pulling out her car keys.* DEAN *sits up in the pool.*)

DEAN. We're serving chicken. I heard you.

JESSICA. Ground lamb and beef.

DEAN. Burgers?

JESSICA. Dean.

DEAN. What?

JESSICA. Make sure you scrub down the grill before you fill it with the charcoal.

DEAN. So I'm in charge this afternoon?

JESSICA. Of the grill. Yes.

DEAN. Yowsers. Big step there, Jess.

JESSICA. I'm trying, okay?

DEAN. Or should I use your secret code name, Agent Designation?

JESSICA. Throwing a party's a big deal for me.

DEAN. Watch, I make it look easy.

JESSICA. Inviting people here is, it's huge.

DEAN. So let me help you.

JESSICA. Oh you are. I left you a long list on the kitchen table.

DEAN. Right next to my leash on the hook inside the door?

JESSICA. Now that's not fair.

DEAN. Neither is micro-managing me.

JESSICA. We just need to be ready, that's all –

DEAN. And we will be. They're my friends. Let me take care of it.

JESSICA. Right, because they are *your* friends.

DEAN. Who will soon be *our* friends. C'mon. Isn't that the point?

JESSICA. Sort of.

DEAN. All you have to do is come home, take a shower, and show up.

JESSICA. Just cross off the list as you go.

DEAN. Ouch, maybe that leash is already chaffing my neck.

JESSICA. I think of stuff that you don't, that's all. It's your house too.

DEAN. I would have asked a band. Tyler knows some guys down at Jensen's who play together.

JESSICA. Those bozos can barely fit their guitars over their beer bellies.

DEAN. And I would have sprung for chicken.

JESSICA. When was the last time you went with me to the grocery store, to see how much chicken costs these days?

DEAN. But it's a party.

> (**DEAN** *climbs out of the pool. He knows he looks good in a swimsuit.*)

I'll make sure you have a fun time tonight, don't worry.

JESSICA. I'm not worried about the fun, you're always fun.

DEAN. I like when you fret.

JESSICA. That's why I make lists.

DEAN. It's sexy.

JESSICA. It is?

DEAN. Uh huh.

> (**JESSICA** *throws him a towel.*)

So are you going to tell me?

JESSICA. Fine. You are in complete and total charge, Dean. Fly like a sparrow. Happy?

DEAN. Not that. Before. This morning. In bed.

JESSICA. Don't.

DEAN. I was getting nervous. We haven't really – *communicated* – like that –

JESSICA. I need to go.

DEAN. Months. We've only been going out a year, and it's been two months.

JESSICA. It was nice.

DEAN. So. Why did you bury your face in the pillow when I tried to talk to you about –?

JESSICA. It's just me. My deal. I can't tell you exactly –

DEAN. So is that going to be it? A comet?

JESSICA. Who knows, right?

DEAN. C'mon Jess. Make me blush. Right now.

> (**JESSICA** *finishes wiping down his chest with the towel.*)

JESSICA. You look like a little boy when you blush.

> (**DEAN** *takes her in his arms and they kiss.*)

DEAN. I missed you like this.

JESSICA. I'm right there next to you, every night.

DEAN. Tell me what you said. Something about your panties?

JESSICA. Never mind about my –

DEAN. How my hands feel on your skin as I take them off, maybe?

JESSICA. Cheesy.

DEAN. I want this morning to happen again, please.

JESSICA. The kids.

DEAN. Morning naptime's magical.

JESSICA. They're already going to be so screwed up, living in my backyard.

DEAN. Am I going to have to interrogate your pillowcase?

JESSICA. I just –

DEAN. Under the heat lamp?

JESSICA. I'd like –

DEAN. Yeah? Tell me what you like.

JESSICA. I'd like to know why you ripped off my panties and stuffed them in your mouth. That's all.

DEAN. Why I –

JESSICA. Yeah, why did you do that?

DEAN. You don't like it.

JESSICA. I didn't say that.

DEAN. Cause the look on your face –

JESSICA. It surprised me.

DEAN. I like surprises.

JESSICA. But why did you stuff them in your mouth? I – I – I've never really seen anything like that, so. That's all.

(Pause.)

Is it the way they feel in your mouth?

DEAN. You mean the texture?

JESSICA. Did you not want to kiss me?

DEAN. You have no idea what you do to me. It's like I want to climb inside of you sometimes.

JESSICA. Okay.

DEAN. And I'm sorry if that's too intense for you to think about, but –

JESSICA. I can handle it.

DEAN. But that's all I've got to offer you right now.

JESSICA. If there's something you want to do for yourself, I'm not going to say no.

DEAN. Don't you have silverware waiting to roll?

JESSICA. You are in charge.

DEAN. Yep, I've got tables to set up, lanterns to hang.

JESSICA. Lanterns?

DEAN. You have no idea what awaits you. Everyone's heard me brag about you for so long now.

JESSICA. Oh don't add to the pressure.

DEAN. What? They know we are a couple now.

JESSICA. A couple, huh?

DEAN. And couples say yes to invitations from other couples.

JESSICA. It sounds cozy.

DEAN. Cozy's a good word for it. We'll be ready when you get home.

JESSICA. Excuse me. "We"?

DEAN. I have a team to mobilize.

JESSICA. Yeah, good luck with that.

>   *(A moment.)*

Jim and Sandy say hello.

DEAN. Jim and Sandy –?

JESSICA. The Finns.

DEAN. Right. Wow. How are they?

JESSICA. Good. He's volunteering extra days down at the hospital, but she's still teaching. They asked how you were doing and I told them you were keeping your chin up and still out looking –

DEAN. My chin's up.

JESSICA. They asked if you'd talked to Charlotte, if she knew you were back in town, living with me.

DEAN. Charlotte Finn?

JESSICA. They asked.

DEAN. I haven't talked to her in over ten years. Where is she?

JESSICA. They were headed to four o'clock mass, so –

DEAN. How did I come up?

JESSICA. Jim said you wrote an article on the layoffs at the tubing plant.

DEAN. Right. So where's this list?

JESSICA. Kitchen table.

DEAN. Just in case.

JESSICA. Next to the newspaper.

DEAN. Folded open to the jobs page?

JESSICA. It's a column now, not the whole page.

DEAN. Part-time secretaries and cement mixer operators.

JESSICA. It might be open to the sports page.

> *(Starts out along the side of the house, towards her car.)*

You'll just have to check.

DEAN. Where's Nan?

JESSICA. Make sure she's taking those kids –

DEAN. Grandparents.

JESSICA. And there are cases of beer in the garage. We need ice. And she owes me six bucks for handy-wipes.

DEAN. I'll take care of the six bucks.

JESSICA. Oh and I left a green marker between the list and the paper, to cross off as you go, if you want to. You know.

DEAN. Forget about the party.

JESSICA. Why? I'm thrilled. Be back before six. Bye!

DEAN. I still like you a lot.

JESSICA. Duh. But this morning I have the bite marks to prove it.

> *(JESSICA is gone. DEAN looks after her clutching the towel she used to wipe him down. He fiddles with the garbage by the fence, tugging at some of the wrappers, creating more of a mess. He pauses for a moment, then bounds up the stairs into the house.)*

(As the screen door slams behind him, the trailer door opens. **TYLER** *comes out with a sack over his shoulder. He deposits it in the middle of the yard, nearly tipping over into the pool. Inside the trailer, we can dimly hear the sound of a children's program on TV.)*

TYLER. Dean. Dean. Man, are you up yet?

DEAN. *(Off, from the house.)* It's almost noon.

TYLER. I'm on toddler watch. I have no freakin' clue what time means. Are you ready?

DEAN. I think I'm gonna need your help.

(Returns from the house, shirted, holding the list.)

What you got there?

TYLER. One of my kids, trussed up and ready for the city dump.

(Pulls an apple out, bites.)

We're making pie.

DEAN. "We" just got a long and detailed to do list on the table.

TYLER. Yeah, I thought we'd be the heroes of this party tonight.

DEAN. There's a lot to do out here –

TYLER. The men folk, covered in flour and grease.

DEAN. Wanna get on some reality cooking show, do you? Where's the camera?

TYLER. Strapped in above my bed. Naw, c'mon. You and me know how to do this.

DEAN. That's what you said when we streaked across Miller Park with Bernie Kozar's jersey numbers painted on our backs.

TYLER. Dean, my kids are inside watching BuggleLand and you're blabbing about my woeful loyalty to the Cleveland Browns? Let me keep my dignity.

DEAN. Remind me never to go in on Fantasy Football with you.

TYLER. Your mom taught us this shit. It'll be a tribute.

DEAN. Mom paid us ten bucks to spread mulch on the yard.

TYLER. Then my mom – what's the difference whose mom taught us? We need to show 'em how pie is done.

(**TYLER** *is practically straddling the pile of apples.*)

DEAN. Where's Nan?

TYLER. What's Nan got to do with our mastery of the culinary arts?

DEAN. She talks you out of it.

TYLER. Nan loves when I cook.

DEAN. I need all hands on deck today.

TYLER. All she knows how to do is read my credit card number off to the guy at the takeout place.

DEAN. *(Calls in.)* Nan.

TYLER. She had errands to run.

DEAN. Can she pick up some stuff for the party?

TYLER. I can call. Not sure she's gonna have enough time –

DEAN. But she's taking the kids over to your mother's?

TYLER. Her mother's, actually.

DEAN. Her mother?

TYLER. Nan talks to them all the time these days, country club gossip. I stay out of it so they keep talking.

(*Pause.*)

You two were pretty crazy this morning.

DEAN. You heard us?

TYLER. Her yard's pretty tiny.

DEAN. Yeah, well – let's break up this list.

TYLER. Nan's pregnant again.

DEAN. What?

TYLER. Yup. And she digs a nice hot Granny Smith apple pie during the first trimester.

DEAN. How can she be pregnant again?

TYLER. We figure, we've got so much love for these two, too much really –

DEAN. Does all this love come with a matching savings account?

TYLER. Aw, here we go.

DEAN. You told me you and Nan were done with all that when I let you park your tribe in our yard.

TYLER. We thought we were done, believe me.

DEAN. I told Jess, I promised her.

TYLER. Buddy, I know.

DEAN. Christmas. You'd be gone by Christmas. Her family's coming down to stay with us.

TYLER. Okay, let me see that list of yours.

DEAN. And I can't meet her family with my best friend's girl breastfeeding her newborn out the kitchen window. Are you listening to me, buddy?

TYLER. Look, Nan's parents barely remember to send our kids birthday cards. But her brother and his wife the barren psychologist get season tickets for "Jersey Boys" when it comes to Cleveland. I don't need you giving her more grief.

DEAN. It's not Nan's fault. She didn't make assurances. She couldn't just put a condom on once in a while.

TYLER. Are you Coach Kandrac? Are we seventeen again all of a sudden?

DEAN. I trust you when you make promises.

TYLER. *(Pats trailer.)* Tell your lady friend it wasn't our fault, it's the mojo of this nest here. Never lets us down.

DEAN. How could it? It takes three steps to get from the kitchen to the bed.

TYLER. We get alone inside and nothing holds us back.

DEAN. And why not another, right?

TYLER. Don't be jealous.

DEAN. We're thirty now, Tyler.

TYLER. Ooh, I'm so scared. Age ain't nuthin' but a number.

DEAN. Be an adult. Make a plan and see it through.

TYLER. That's funny coming from you.

DEAN. Look, I can't deal with you today. Jess will be dazzled by what we can pull off.

TYLER. Sure she will. We got your back and you have ours.

DEAN. Think so, huh?

TYLER. C'mon, Nan and me work it out. Hope with us.

DEAN. I'm trying to make a team here, okay?

TYLER. I'm with you on the lady friend.

DEAN. Jess thought you were both working on finding real jobs so you could save some actual money.

TYLER. I'm on it.

DEAN. I don't see you on it. What I see is a satellite dish on the roof of your trailer and a pile of Brunswick County apples you probably paid organic prices for.

> (**TYLER** *finishes his apple and pitches the core towards the clutter near the fence.*)

TYLER. But these are the juiciest. She's embarrassed.

DEAN. Jeez, back to Nan's feelings.

TYLER. She knows your lady friend is getting too old to have kids.

> (*Snaps.*)

What do you want me to say, Dean? Sorry I'm having another baby with my girl? I'm not going to do that. We're crazy happy. And despite what Jessica thinks, being a dad is the greatest thing that's ever happened to me.

DEAN. I just hope your kids eventually agree with you.

TYLER. Don't heap your parent bullshit on me, Dean. I was right there when your dad took off, that's old news –

DEAN. I'm not even thinking about him.

TYLER. And I do have money coming in.

DEAN. Being a mail carrier's like being the milkman. Both endangered species.

TYLER. Hey but I go somewhere every morning, don't I? And I get to be home right now watching my kids watch TV. Best friend's fifty feet away in his own house. This is the life, buddy.

DEAN. Your life. We have plans too.

TYLER. She has plans.

DEAN. No, Jess and me –

TYLER. You have a football schedule. Look, this city's going to reinvent itself in the next couple of years –

DEAN. You keep saying that.

TYLER. – And if we just keep plugging along, eyes peeled for the right opportunity –

DEAN. We can make it happen for ourselves.

TYLER. Exactly. That's our Moment.

DEAN. How can you be so optimistic?

TYLER. We know how this place works, Dean. It's our home.

DEAN. Look, I already did this once. I came back here because I believed there were still opportunities. And look what happened.

TYLER. Newspapers swallow each other up all the time, Dean. Nobody reads. Don't take it personally.

DEAN. It's the hometown paper. They asked me to come run it. I didn't apply, they asked me.

(*Pause.*)

Jeez, when did we start talking so old?

(**TYLER** *starts to laugh, breaking the tension.* **DEAN** *joins him.*)

TYLER. I mean it. We'll figure it out and go. Thanksgiving.

DEAN. You know who comes into her restaurant? The Finns.

TYLER. Charlotte Finn?

DEAN. Her parents.

TYLER. Wow.

DEAN. I know.

TYLER. God, I was such a tool senior year.

DEAN. You just didn't know when to shut up. Hasn't changed.

TYLER. Well she was just as screwed up.

DEAN. Nah, Charlotte was okay. Girls were nasty to her.

TYLER. I suppose.

DEAN. She still must have got out, into the world.

TYLER. Yeah, Charlotte Finn's probably the head of some big corporation someplace with its own road.

DEAN. No, she's probably a journalist like me. We made plans together. Bounced ideas. Gave each other pep talks.

TYLER. Then she's giving Lois Lane a run for her money, huh?

DEAN. I hope.

TYLER. See? Isn't that easy? *Hope.*

(*Pause.*)

DEAN. Do you still have that marinade recipe?

TYLER. What, the black pepper soy honey?

DEAN. Can you throw some together?

TYLER. And there are some secret ingredients –

DEAN. I'm sure Nan has gummy worms.

TYLER. Sure. Anything.

DEAN. (*Crosses an item off the list.*) Well that's one.

(*Flips to the second page.*)

She's got it together, you know? She knows her life.

TYLER. So do you.

DEAN. Not lately.

TYLER. It's right here. Show her who is boss.

DEAN. C'mon.

TYLER. I mean it. We'll help you.

DEAN. Let's just get through the party tonight, okay?

TYLER. Now you're talking. Isn't that enough, sometimes? A really awesome burger, a beer, and some pie with your friends?

> (**DEAN** *dumps the sack of apples into the pool, where they land with a splash. He tosses the sack aside towards the clutter by the fence.*)

DEAN. No pie. We'll bob for apples later.

End of Scene

Scene Two

(Later. The grill is set up. A cooler is by the side of the house. **NAN** *is rolling silverware and placing the napkins into a brightly decorated basket.* **TYLER** *sets up lawn chairs, around the tables.)*

NAN. I left wax in her bathroom.

TYLER. What were you doing up there?

NAN. She was gone, so I took a bath in the big tub. Lit some candles.

TYLER. Where was I?

NAN. You took the girls to the bike show, so I could be alone.

TYLER. I'm nice.

NAN. Sure are. And I laid out here on the OSU blanket we got from my brother, right here by the tree stump. It was the clearest night all summer. As wide as I could see.

TYLER. Far, babe. As far as you could see.

NAN. Shows how much you know, you weren't even here. The sky wrapped itself around me, close enough that I could practically reach the stars. No light from the other houses. No smoke stacks from the factory downtown. Just me and the sky and possibility, wide as can be. Everything in life just felt so correct, you know?

TYLER. I do.

NAN. Then I remembered the candles and they were this big pool of wax on the floor. I used turpentine to scrape it off. So it's my fault.

TYLER. We need our own place. Three kids, potty training, kindergarten?

NAN. You're so eager for them to grow up.

TYLER. They are growing, babe.

NAN. I know, it's just. I like it here.

TYLER. Well I promised Dean.

NAN. Dean, right.

TYLER. And don't you want our own place again?

NAN. Of course, because you do –

TYLER. And so your parents can visit again, right?

NAN. No. I like not having a pile of bills stuffed into a mason jar. I like not paying rent to the downstairs neighbors. It's our home, Tyler, for our family. We *chose* it. And I like being around Jessica, she's so pretty and successful and put together.

TYLER. Babe, you're a great mom. We do fine on our own, you don't have to worry about that.

NAN. I'm not. I just like feeling decent. And real. You should hear my parents, like jobs are everywhere and we're just being lazy.

TYLER. No thanks.

    (NAN holds up her basket of silverware.)

NAN. Isn't this cool, Dean?

    (DEAN has entered, bringing down a bag of charcoal from the garage. The list sticks out of his back pocket and he wears a cooking apron.)

DEAN. Festive. Nice job.

NAN. Why thank you very much.

DEAN. We have to hang the lanterns yet –

TYLER. I'm on it.

DEAN. I pulled the ladder out from the garage.

NAN. What about me?

DEAN. There's a tablecloth up on the counter.

    (NAN leaps up, already in motion.)

NAN. I'll bring it down.

DEAN. You lined the basket with my newspaper.

NAN. You're a thumbtack. You're so sharp. I was hoping to surprise you. Everyone will see your old byline when they pick up their spoon.

DEAN. Where did you find it?

NAN. There's a whole stack of issues out in the recycle bin. We can't pretend it didn't happen, so why don't we celebrate what you got to do?

TYLER. Sweet idea, babe.

NAN. Ooh, I'm so proud of it. It all happens for a reason, y'know. Tyler walked around like a deflated balloon when you lived in Chicago.

> (*NAN exits into the house.* **TYLER** *watches* **DEAN** *as he takes the basket to the table.*)

DEAN. Do you need help with the ladder?

TYLER. It's okay to still be mad.

DEAN. It's been almost three months. I'm sliding from mad to bitter. And there's enough bitterness around here. Remember Jack Langley, his opinion column?

TYLER. Sure the funny old guy on the local station.

DEAN. He wrote this piece about wandering sons, picking up and leaving home, going off for college and never coming back. It was around the time the coalmines closed over in Sharon, and all those jobs were just gone. And you know, Jack didn't blame the dried-up community colleges and all those vacant storefronts on Grove Street. He didn't even name the corporation that closed the mines down. He blamed us, the sons who left. We were supposed to come back and keep it going, plant our feet back down in the soil. Take over the fight from our fathers.

TYLER. Not my old man. No thanks.

DEAN. You are exactly who Jack Langley wants, you stayed here, stuck by this town through it all. So maybe this is his revenge, you think? When I told my boss in Chicago I was coming back to take over this newspaper, he didn't even try to hide the smirk when I talked about my "roots" here. He knew I was doomed. You're an uppity traitor if you leave, and a jerk that can't cut it out there when you come back. And having the

Youngstown Chronicle just stroll in and fire my whole staff –

(A moment.)

Sorry. Just getting the bitter out of my system before Jess gets back.

TYLER. Well, this is gonna be one hell of a party.

DEAN. I've gotta be good at something, right? Grilling burgers could be it.

(DEAN starts scraping the grill clean. NAN re-enters with the tablecloths and two beers.)

NAN. Sun's thinking about coming down. Cocktail hour.

TYLER. Babe.

NAN. Mom and Pops will have started, why shouldn't we?

(TYLER kisses her as he takes the beers. DEAN watches them as he scrapes.)

DEAN. Can you two promise not to talk about the baby tonight?

NAN. Right, it's bad luck.

TYLER. Whoa, I'm the first of the gang to make three. I gotta brag.

NAN. This is Jess' party with Dean.

DEAN. Thank you.

NAN. We'll have our own bash.

TYLER. Ah, baby showers are old news. And if Mike brings any of his home-brewed juice, all bets are off.

NAN. Still my bad boy. No wonder my mother hisses at your mother from the front pew at church.

(NAN takes a tiny sip of TYLER's beer, enlists him to help her with the tablecloths.)

DEAN. What are you going to tag this one, Nan?

NAN. Sure as hell not *Dean*.

DEAN. Isn't it for migratory purposes?

NAN. Funny.

DEAN. C'mon, you always have a name. Mildred?

NAN. Yuck.

DEAN. How about Taylor?

NAN. I don't think so.

TYLER. Who says it's a girl?

NAN. You make baby girls, stud. Own it.

TYLER. We're not naming anybody right now.

DEAN. Well, I have a long list of names from your ex-girlfriends –

TYLER. Spoken like a true wingman.

NAN. Tyler thinks we jinx it every time by only talking girl names.

DEAN. Ah. A son.

TYLER. Shut it.

DEAN. Your spitting image, except he'll actually fly-fish.

TYLER. My uncle took us more than that one time.

NAN. And you stuck your finger with the hook, nearly passed out.

TYLER. Shush.

DEAN. "C'mere, boy. Water's nothing to be afraid of – "

(**DEAN** *splashes* **TYLER** *with pool water.*)

TYLER. Buddy, I'd quit it!

DEAN. "You think you're going to melt, like a witch?"

(**NAN** *laughs like Margaret Hamilton and claps.*)

TYLER. I said shut it. I'm excited – I get to be really excited for once – about the possibility of a freakin' heir to my empire.

NAN. If we got married, you'd already have two heirs.

TYLER. We're married emotionally.

DEAN. Yeah, Jess and I might beat you to the altar, buddy.

TYLER. Ha. Not with the sustained silent reading y'all are doing upstairs.

NAN. Ooh.

DEAN. You don't know what you're hearing –

TYLER. Don't I? I've got plenty to show for my relationship.

(**DEAN** *slaps the BIG DICK sign on the trailer.*)

DEAN. Yeah, what an empire.

TYLER. Maybe you need a checklist for that too, huh, Dean?

(**TYLER** *and* **DEAN** *scuffle loudly. A toddler calls for her mother inside.*)

NAN. Thanks fellas. Coming sugarplum.

TYLER. I'll get her, babe.

NAN. No, they have to go over to their grandma's house anyway.

DEAN. We're just poking fun at each other.

NAN. What else have I been hearing all these years?

TYLER. Don't be mad.

NAN. His girlfriend's training some kids to do her job on a Sunday. Least we can do is make it look like we did something too. Hang the friggin' lanterns.

(*Turns into the trailer.*)

I'm bringing grape juice, then we're putting on your fancy hat.

(**NAN** *closes the trailer door behind her.* **TYLER** *drinks his beer as* **DEAN** *consults the list, makes another check.*)

DEAN. Did you talk to her?

TYLER. We'll start looking.

DEAN. Good. You've brainwashed her. She'd never leave this yard if she could.

TYLER. She likes your lady friend. Maybe she should throw us out.

DEAN. I'm not throwing you –

TYLER. Naw, point taken.

DEAN. You don't do yourself any favors keeping that BIG DICK sign stuck to the back of your trailer.

TYLER. Nothing wrong with a little advertising.

DEAN. Yeah, that's a smart reason. C'mon, what are you trying to prove?

TYLER. Is this a Jessica question, or –?

DEAN. *(Imitating* **JESSICA**.*)* "I just want to know why you keep it where I have to look at it every single day. That's all."

TYLER. Wait. Let me get my sauce.

> (**TYLER** *scurries up the steps into the trailer for a second, comes back with a bowl and a stirring spoon.)*

DEAN. Honey soy chipotle pepper? That tar?

TYLER. *Black* pepper. Yeah, once I add the oil there, keep stirring, or it gets these clumps.

DEAN. Phew, I hope it doesn't smell like unwashed dog cooking on the grill.

TYLER. It's gonna be delicious.

DEAN. Who's going to hang the lanterns if you're –

TYLER. Well, what are you doing?

DEAN. I'm supposed to be man-ing the grill!

TYLER. Baby'll be fine for five minutes. Get the lanterns. I'll hold the ladder.

DEAN. Wow, this one must be an epic.

> (**DEAN** *brings a string of paper lanterns down from the house and they string them up, dangerously teetering on the lawn furniture and tree stump to do it.)*

TYLER. Me and Nan are driving back from Florida, bringing the stuff her aunt left when she died, playing Christian stations the whole way –

DEAN. Wait, why Christian stations?

TYLER. Can we just talk BIG DICK?

DEAN. Go.

TYLER. We stop at this place called Jasper. It wasn't even a town, just a couple houses and a general store. Nan wants some licorice, so I head in to pay for gas and get some. There's this gal with an alligator tattoo, I kid you not, eating a swan coming down her forearm, rings me up. She's got on these flip-flops and every step is that sound of the rubber hitting the bottom of her little feet. So I bring my cup of coffee up to the counter, and all of a sudden she's there, leaning into me with a jug of milk. "I think you need some cream."

DEAN. Wow.

TYLER. Now she's got to be smack dab between Nan and Jessica's age. Old enough to know exactly what she's doing, but young enough not to really give a fuck – *freak* – if it's bad for her – the right age, you know? Nan's maybe fifty feet away, in the car, out like a light.

DEAN. So where did you take her?

TYLER. Excuse me?

DEAN. C'mon.

TYLER. Where did I take her? I told her I drink my coffee black, got the fuck – the *freak* – away from her, you asshole.

DEAN. Not how you tell me a story, buddy.

TYLER. What are you talking about?

DEAN. You got the fuck away from her? You?

TYLER. I'm not some pussy hound.

DEAN. But you can still look –

TYLER. I was looking.

DEAN. And so was she?

TYLER. Hell yeah. And she was sweating boredom, alright?

DEAN. Yeah, more than alright.

TYLER. So she flip-flops back behind the counter and finally rings me up. My wallets out, I've got one eye on Nan in the car, the other on that damn swan. When she hands me back the change, she pulls out that sticker from the rack behind her, and it says BIG DICK. She slaps it down into my hand with the quarters, and says "I think you need this more than I do."

DEAN. And you still didn't go for it?

TYLER. The sticker's the story.

(Stirs a moment, then.)

What the hell do you think I am?

DEAN. A guy who knows where the bathroom lock is in a public rest stop.

TYLER. Years ago, before I met –

DEAN. Nan. Right. So that was it?

TYLER. I forgot the licorice. Nan pouted all the way to the Ohio border.

(Grins.)

Then we made up.

(Pause.)

DEAN. Jess and I talked about getting matching tattoos once.

TYLER. Ink's not the same as a ring.

DEAN. Neither are baby girls.

TYLER. I still get chances and I turn them down, but I keep the story. Maybe if you had more gals like BIG DICK, maybe you'd be certain about your lady friend.

DEAN. How did you explain that sign to Nan anyway?

TYLER. I told her you gave it to me.

DEAN. And she bought that?

TYLER. Sure. Besides, we played soccer together. You'd know as well as anybody, right?

(Sticks finger in the bowl.)

Taste this.

(DEAN tastes the marinade.)

DEAN. Sour.

TYLER. Time to raid the pantry.

DEAN. Be careful in there.

TYLER. I need some Grade B maple syrup. Shh.

DEAN. *(Back to the list.)* Hurry up. I'm running out of time.

TYLER. We're doing a fine job. Looks presentable.

DEAN. Almost.

(TYLER climbs the stairs into the house. A light turns on in the kitchen. When he's alone, DEAN pulls out a pair of women's underwear from the apron pocket and holds them in his hand.)

(JESSICA enters from the side of the house.)

JESSICA. There are balloons tied to my mailbox. Balloons.

DEAN. Yup.

JESSICA. Grill's prepped. Table's nearly set.

DEAN. *(Holds up his list.)* Check Check Check.

JESSICA. Lanterns –

DEAN. One sec.

(Dashes over to the side of the house with power cord, leaving the underwear on the tree stump. Plugs in the cable.)

Boo-yeah.

(The lanterns light up, casting a glow.)

JESSICA. My busy bee.

DEAN. I deviated, but still got it all done.

JESSICA. I am very –

DEAN. Impressed? Dazzled?

JESSICA. – Happy. We might actually pull this off.

(A moment.)

Are those mine?

DEAN. Uh-huh. I took them. After we –

JESSICA. This morning?

DEAN. Uh-huh.

JESSICA. And you've been carrying them around?

DEAN. A memento.

JESSICA. We'll do it again.

DEAN. I certainly hope so.

JESSICA. *(Examines them.)* These aren't the softest. Cheap elastic, pinches my skin.

DEAN. They feel nice to me.

(Pause.)

JESSICA. Why don't you put them on?

DEAN. Why would I do that?

JESSICA. You can if you want to. I don't mind.

DEAN. That's not for me.

JESSICA. But snooping around in my room?

DEAN. Our room.

JESSICA. I'm not complaining you took them – if you need something so you can feel close to me, when I'm at work – a secret. I don't know.

DEAN. Don't you think I'm whipped enough without wearing your clothes too?

JESSICA. Dean.

DEAN. And here's your precious list back.

(DEAN hands it to her and starts out.)

JESSICA. I want to make you happy, Dean.

DEAN. I'm fine.

JESSICA. If you can't be excited about your job right now, be excited about us.

DEAN. It's not a job, it was a career. There's a difference.

JESSICA. I'll do anything you want. I told myself I'd try anything you want.

DEAN. You gave yourself a pep talk?

JESSICA. I saw the look on your face this morning. You were wild.

DEAN. Wearing your underwear's not going to turn me on.

JESSICA. What are you afraid of?

DEAN. The kids are still here –

JESSICA. All I'm saying, Dean, is that I would be open to helping you, explore, whatever it is you want to explore.

DEAN. I have no clue what I want. Remember? That's why I stick with you, Jess. Eventually, you'll get around to telling me, right?

(JESSICA kisses him.)

Hey babe.

JESSICA. It looks real sweet out here.

DEAN. Burgers are on a tray in the kitchen, veggies are cut. Your casserole's in the oven –

JESSICA. You made my casserole?

DEAN. Followed the recipe. Even turned on the heat this time.

JESSICA. We are ready for a party.

DEAN. Tyler's making this famous marinade he's got, infamous really, and Nan set the table.

JESSICA. You got them to pitch in?

DEAN. They wanted to help.

JESSICA. Go Team Dean.

> *(They kiss again,* JESSICA *pulling* DEAN *over on to one of the tables.)*

DEAN. It wasn't a fluke, don't worry.

> *(A moment.)*

How's the restaurant?

JESSICA. Yapping little monkey tykes strapped to highchairs, shrieking about French toast.

DEAN. Sunday afternoon.

JESSICA. We better get rid of these coupon offers, otherwise I might have to behead any parties of six or more.

> *(*DEAN *pulls a chair over for her to put her feet on, for him to rub.)*

DEAN. Decapitation. I'll get you a beer.

JESSICA. Thanks. Did you fill the ice back up in the fridge?

DEAN. Jess.

JESSICA. The new kids are gonna be fine, they just need to practice carrying more than two glasses in each hand at a time. And I ran into the Finns again. Charlotte was with them.

> *(*DEAN *brings her a cold beer from the cooler.)*

DEAN. Charlotte's here?

JESSICA. Standing in the parking lot, just in from Portland.

DEAN. She lives in Portland?

JESSICA. I guess so. Her dad's turning sixty this weekend, so –

DEAN. Did she seem happy?

JESSICA. Sure. She's here with a guy, married.

> (Pause.)

She asked about you right away, how you were doing. Sandy must have told her you'd taken up with me.

DEAN. Taken up with?

JESSICA. You know. Anyway, she remembered you.

DEAN. Charlotte got me through SATs.

JESSICA. Yeah, she seems sharp.

DEAN. We had stuff in common.

> (Pause.)

JESSICA. Yeah, well, those balloons. Nobody's going to miss this place.

DEAN. Everyone knows where you live –

JESSICA. Where you live.

DEAN. Now I took the liberty of getting some citronella candles.

JESSICA. Citronella, ooh.

DEAN. So we all don't get eaten alive out here.

JESSICA. I definitely didn't think of citronella.

DEAN. So I'm gonna go get them from the garage and put them out.

JESSICA. "Cool."

DEAN. Then I get to have a beer.

JESSICA. You deserve one.

> (DEAN *hides the empty bottles from before in the cluttered fence as he crosses towards the house.*)

I invited them over for the party.

DEAN. Who?

JESSICA. Charlotte Finn and her husband.

DEAN. Why did you do that?

JESSICA. They're a couple, we're having a party with other couples.

DEAN. I don't want her coming here.

JESSICA. That's harsh –

DEAN. It's a bad idea.

JESSICA. What's the big deal?

DEAN. Tonight's about my friends becoming your friends. Ours. It's not a reunion.

JESSICA. He said they'd probably only show up for dessert.

DEAN. Enough time for Charlotte Finn to tell us how she's breaking news and reporting up and down the West Coast –

JESSICA. She doesn't seem that type.

DEAN. Bragging about the politicians she talks to, who all know her on a first name basis –

JESSICA. Aren't you curious about your old friend's life?

DEAN. She wasn't really my friend.

JESSICA. You just told me you were friends –

DEAN. We were study partners. If anything, she was competition.

(A moment.)

I don't want her here. Not right now. Please.

JESSICA. Why are you so tense?

DEAN. How am I going to explain how I got stuck back here?

JESSICA. Stuck?

DEAN. – And Tyler's going to hit the roof when he sees her.

JESSICA. Tyler isn't throwing this party with me, you are.

DEAN. We all have a history, that's all.

JESSICA. You could say that about anyone in this town.

(Pause.)

She's bringing a dessert.

DEAN. Woo-hoo.

JESSICA. She seems fun. It's just a party.

DEAN. Yeah, I guess that's all that matters.

> (DEAN *exits around the side of the house.* JESSICA *takes a sip of beer, looks down at her list, and crumples it up.*)

> (NAN *has entered from the trailer, sets down her diaper bag.*)

NAN. Just taking my girls.

JESSICA. *(Takes a longer swig of beer.)* Good. I'm getting drunk tonight. My new servers are rubbing off on me.

NAN. They talked about her my freshman year. And she just walked the halls with this little smile on her face, like she knew a secret and wasn't telling. There were lots of stories, and she never denied anything. I think she liked the attention.

JESSICA. Who are you talking about?

NAN. Charlotte Finn. Are you sure it was really her?

JESSICA. You'll see for yourself. She's coming.

> *(A moment.)*

Are those apples floating in the pool?

End of Scene

Scene Three

(Later, nightfall. Party is ready to start: the lanterns glow, candles are lit at each of the tables, all very elegant – except a string of garish purple lights that adorn the trailer. JESSICA is arranging the table of food by the house, near the cooler. TYLER is fishing the apples back out of the pool and into the sack.)

JESSICA. It's just, the pool takes up so much space.

TYLER. I get it, Jessica.

JESSICA. But I like having it here for them, your girls.

TYLER. Me too.

JESSICA. Nobody's bringing kids tonight.

TYLER. Do you want me to drain it too?

JESSICA. No. I just, who's going to get drunk enough to stick their head in dirty water and bob –?

TYLER. Wait until you meet my friends.

JESSICA. Right. Ha ha.

TYLER. Or I could grab that plastic slide from next door, Dean gets the hose. We make a slip and slide.

JESSICA. Dean knows it's not that kind of party. Sorry.

(Straightens a tablecloth.)

What's he thinking?

TYLER. Actually, Dean tried to talk me out of it.

JESSICA. Your children play here.

TYLER. My girls can eat a little dirt. Dean wanted to bake them into pies. The apples, not my girls.

JESSICA. I love apple pie.

TYLER. Right, and he knew that so he thought it would be really cool to put on the baking hats, get out the rolling pin –

JESSICA. *(Warm.)* He's crazy.

TYLER. But I was, as Dean would put it, undeterred. Sorry.

JESSICA. Maybe you can still make one.

TYLER. Oh I don't know.

JESSICA. I bet it would smell pretty great, with the windows open.

TYLER. Yeah, Dean's pretty fast on his feet in a kitchen, but he's had so many responsibilities today. I think we're out of time tonight, Jessica.

JESSICA. You can call me Jess, you know. Nan does.

(**TYLER** *lifts the sack of apples over his shoulder.*)

TYLER. Can I take them inside now?

JESSICA. Sure, I'll have your next beer ready.

TYLER. Swell.

(*He takes the sack into the trailer, closes the door.* **JESSICA** *pulls out another beer and opens it for him, decides to drink it herself.* **DEAN** *enters from the house, collared shirt and jeans, holding the tinfoil-covered platter of burgers for the grill.*)

DEAN. Hope you like spicy.

JESSICA. How spicy?

DEAN. His marinade might've singed my fingertips off.

(*At the table.*)

Where do you want –?

JESSICA. I guess the burgers go on the end.

DEAN. Sure.

JESSICA. You decide. You're the chef.

DEAN. Did you see the buns I got? Extra thick so they really soak up all the juice.

(*She's staring.*)

What'd I do?

JESSICA. Nothing. Why do you think you did anything wrong?

DEAN. Default.

JESSICA. Hold my hand.

DEAN. Was that on my list?

JESSICA. You've been putting this together all day, let's just relax until folks show up. You've earned it, baby. What? I can't call you "baby"?

>   (**DEAN** *takes her hand.*)

DEAN. Put down the beer. C'mon.

>   (**JESSICA** *gives him her other hand.* **DEAN** *takes them both in his, blows on them.*)

JESSICA. Stop it.

DEAN. Shh.

JESSICA. That tickles, Dean.

DEAN. How do you keep them so soft, touching food and wiping down tables every day?

JESSICA. That job's not who I am.

DEAN. Your hands are.

JESSICA. Can't we just sit here together? I'm feeling pretty crazy.

DEAN. You are, huh?

JESSICA. I can still smell you on me.

DEAN. What are you trying to prove?

JESSICA. Find out.

>   (*Pause.*)

DEAN. So I was thinking about what you said.

JESSICA. Yeah?

DEAN. Jess. That you would be willing –

JESSICA. To explore?

DEAN. Yeah, so I'm done taking directions from you. I'm telling you exactly what I want.

JESSICA. Ha, you are so silly.

DEAN. God, haven't I earned it today? C'mon.

JESSICA. Sorry.

DEAN. I want you to give me something close to you, close to you right now.

JESSICA. Anything –

DEAN. Take them off for me. Right here. Take them off. Now.

> (*JESSICA quickly slides her panties off underneath her skirt, stepping out of them.*)

JESSICA. Here you go.

DEAN. Just like that?

JESSICA. You asked.

DEAN. Wow.

JESSICA. Now what are you going to do with them?

DEAN. I, um –

JESSICA. Because I have some ideas.

DEAN. You do.

JESSICA. Why don't you put them on?

DEAN. Huh.

JESSICA. I know you're thinking about it.

DEAN. Stop trying to control it.

JESSICA. There they are. You have to want to try it, right? Be honest about it. With me. Here.

> (*JESSICA holds them out.*)

DEAN. It doesn't work that way.

JESSICA. Who says?

DEAN. I'm not –

JESSICA. You'll feel so sexy, I promise. Some days, these make all the difference.

DEAN. Just let me tell you what I want.

JESSICA. Don't pout about it. I want you do to it, okay?

> (**DEAN** *grabs the panties from her.*)

DEAN. It doesn't matter anyway.

JESSICA. Dean, do it.

DEAN. Fine. Whatever you say.

> (*Ducks behind the grill, undoes his pants and pulls them off.*)

I feel like an idiot.

JESSICA. No one's coming. Hurry. Now give me yours.

> *(Hidden by the grill,* DEAN *slides the panties up to his waist, quickly refastens his pants. Holds out his boxer briefs.)*

DEAN. What, a trade?

JESSICA. If you need them back, you'll know where to look.

> *(*JESSICA *takes his briefs and slides them up on under her skirt. They both adjust to the new reality between them.)*

DEAN. Why the hell am I doing this?

JESSICA. We are doing this. Kiss me.

> *(He kisses her.)*

Harder.

> *(Again.)*

I like you a lot.

DEAN. Duh.

> *(*JESSICA *exits into the house.)*

> *(*DEAN *sits on the tree stump, and rubs his pants against it, feeling the sensation under his jeans. Despite himself.)*

> *(*TYLER *enters, also spruced up a bit. He has an old portable stereo.)*

TYLER. Hey buddy. Whatcha doing?

> *(*DEAN *leaps up, grabs the tongs.)*

DEAN. Grilling man. Ready for some grilling?

TYLER. You know I be.

DEAN. The marinade is stellar.

TYLER. Sweet-talking the sauce is what I do best.

> *(They clink beers.* DEAN *lights up the grill as* TYLER *plugs in the stereo.)*

DEAN. Let's get this fire going. Yeah.

TYLER. You and lady friend are looking pretty cozy now.

DEAN. Think so?

TYLER. It's nice to see's all.

DEAN. I don't want to be a sad man.

TYLER. Does any of this look sad to you? Wait.

> *(Flips a switch. The disco lights swirl around the patio.)*

Now that will keep us dancing.

DEAN. Did you steal that from my dorm room?

TYLER. Nah, you're back home, Dean.

DEAN. Yeah. Tyler, Jess invited –

> *(**NAN** has appeared in the doorway to the trailer, dressed to kill.)*

NAN. Me and this zipper have finally come to terms. Play that mix CD I gave you.

DEAN. Buddy –

TYLER. *(Presses buttons on the stereo.)* DJ coming right up. Let's see if I can remember how –

DEAN. You made a mix CD?

NAN. Last night, we found a box in the back of his truck. Why not, right?

DEAN. Can't wait.

NAN. If I'm going to squeeze another wailing banshee into this world next year, I'm dancing my freakin' heels off before I do. C'mon baby.

TYLER. Here we go.

> *(Music plays, Cake's "The Distance".)*

NAN. That's what I'm talking about.

TYLER. You still move, babe. Look at her, Dean.

DEAN. I'm watching. Tyler, Jess told me she invited –

TYLER. Did you ever think her body could still move like that?

NAN. Here's hoping –

TYLER. Forever.

NAN. Show me what you can do, baby stud.

> (**TYLER** *joins her.* **NAN** *takes another sip of his beer.* **DEAN** *begins laying out burgers on the grill, watching them. He starts dancing alongside them with his grill tongs, adjusting himself in the underwear.*)

> (**CHARLOTTE FINN** *appears along the side of the house, overdressed for a backyard barbeque. She carries a small pastry box.*)

CHARLOTTE. And I forgot to pack my dancing shoes. Damn.

> (*Stop. The CD starts skipping in the stereo.* **NAN** *races over to stop it.*)

NAN. Friggin CDs.

CHARLOTTE. Is the party over?

NAN. You're first.

CHARLOTTE. Well I guess the early bird will get the worm.

TYLER. Charlotte Finn?

CHARLOTTE. I'm afraid so. Hello.

TYLER. What are you doing in our backyard?

CHARLOTTE. I came to see Dean. I'm invited.

DEAN. Jess invited her. Hey there, Charlotte.

CHARLOTTE. Hey there yourself, Dean. I barely recognize you.

DEAN. Hair's longer, otherwise –

CHARLOTTE. That must be it. Here you are, standing in the middle of – suburbia.

DEAN. Yeah, we've come a long way from that corner table at McKinley Memorial Library, huh?

CHARLOTTE. Already been there. Mrs. O'Donnell says hello.

TYLER. Dean, what's going on here?

> (*Pause.*)

CHARLOTTE. I can't believe I'm back here again.

DEAN. It's different, right?

CHARLOTTE. I passed this house five times. Barely recognized the roads without all the trees they cut down.

DEAN. This town's got a tractor beam like the Death Star.

CHARLOTTE. It's not so bad. Where did you find that song?

NAN. Good taste.

CHARLOTTE. It takes me back. *(Tries to dance.)* Turn it back on.

NAN. It's party music, not talking music.

DEAN. I know you didn't bake dessert.

CHARLOTTE. No, I'm still useless near a stove. I brought donuts. Portlanders are obsessed with donuts.

NAN. My daughters love donuts.

CHARLOTTE. I spend a lot time standing outside Voodoo Donuts, wondering how long the line will take.

(*Turns to* **TYLER.**)

Daughters, Tyler?

TYLER. I need another beer.

CHARLOTTE. I also brought some whiskey. It's sitting on the seat of the Volvo out front.

TYLER. I like beer.

NAN. You love whiskey.

CHARLOTTE. I can go get it –

TYLER. How did this happen? Dean?

CHARLOTTE. It's been a long time, Tyler.

TYLER. Yeah, we thought we lost you to the big bad world out there, Charlotte Finn.

CHARLOTTE. I never belonged here in the first place. Nothing to lose.

TYLER. And it's like you just came back from the convenient store buying milk.

CHARLOTTE. The window's down, so. I'll go –

TYLER. I got the whiskey. You came to see Dean.

> (**TYLER** *goes off alongside the house.* **CHARLOTTE** *holds up her donuts.*)

CHARLOTTE. Where do they go?

DEAN. On the table, by the card marked "sweets."

CHARLOTTE. Look at you, playing host. *(Re: food.)* Did you really make deviled eggs?

DEAN. We're ready for a free for all.

CHARLOTTE. You fit in so well here. This isn't crazy, is it?

DEAN. It doesn't have to be.

CHARLOTTE. *(A moment.)* My dad's using the same tongs. He loves them.

DEAN. Yeah, I'm taking some time off to clear my head, strategize my next step, and really make it count.

CHARLOTTE. It's all you can do sometimes.

DEAN. And I'm figuring out the other stuff too.

CHARLOTTE. She's hardly "stuff" Dean. I got married. Did you ever think that was possible?

DEAN. I hoped.

CHARLOTTE. *(Turns to* **NAN.***)* I went to school with these boys.

NAN. I know who you are. I was three years behind you.

CHARLOTTE. Oh. Right.

NAN. I'm Nan. Mother of the daughters.

CHARLOTTE. You were gymnastics, right?

NAN. Yeah.

CHARLOTTE. You won trophies.

NAN. I did. Yes, that was me.

DEAN. Sharp memory.

CHARLOTTE. I read the paper as fast as my dad could finish a section, and I always saw your picture.

NAN. We still get Christmas cards from my coach. And I can still do this.

> *(Breaks into a posed stretch.)*

After two baby girls and another on the way.

CHARLOTTE. That's impressive.

DEAN. Are Jim and Sandy thrilled?

CHARLOTTE. Mom's beside herself, conveniently forgetting we need Montana between us to maintain any sense of harmony. I'm just poking around town, seeing who's left.

> (**TYLER** *has re-entered with the bottle of whiskey and a bag of ice.*)

NAN. Have you been to the new mall yet?

CHARLOTTE. Second stop on the first day.

DEAN. Tyler's on some committee to get stimulus money from the state to refurnish it, to attract new stores and restaurants again.

CHARLOTTE. Well that fish tank is spectacular. Makes me want to spend money.

TYLER. I'll take your feedback to the committee.

CHARLOTTE. Are you running for city council next, Tyler?

TYLER. Who knows.

NAN. Did you show your husband?

DEAN. Yeah, Jess said you two look happy.

TYLER. Wait, you got married?

CHARLOTTE. People still do get married. He doesn't know anybody here, so we decided it wasn't essential he come.

TYLER. What are you hiding from us, Charlotte Finn?

CHARLOTTE. Nothing. He's shy and makes clicking noises with his jaw when he's nervous. It's distracting in a group. Can I drink something, please?

TYLER. *(Opening the bottle to pour.)* Breaking the seal on this baby –

CHARLOTTE. I figured, since we're all thirty now, whiskey would be proper etiquette.

> (**TYLER** *hands whiskey to* **CHARLOTTE**, *pours himself some.*)

My hero.

> *(Sisterly to* NAN.*)*

A joke.

NAN. Ha. Right. You're funny.

CHARLOTTE. Not really. Dean, you told me I was. And I assumed you were saying that so I would stop pulling my hair out trying to make you chuckle.

DEAN. Jess should be down any minute.

CHARLOTTE. Are you all living together?

NAN. *(Leans against the trailer.)* This is our house.

CHARLOTTE. And there's a pool. So you split all this with Dean?

TYLER. It's good.

CHARLOTTE. Still linked at the hip by your chain wallets.

TYLER. It's not – none of this is all neat and tidy and set, you know.

CHARLOTTE. Yeah, I bet you clean out the eave spouts.

DEAN. It's not –

TYLER. What?

DEAN. So bad. Or permanent, okay?

NAN. Where are you going, Dean?

TYLER. Yeah, where are you gonna go?

CHARLOTTE. I might be high from the Citronella candles but you seem genuinely content to me.

DEAN. Yeah, I love going to car shows and swim meets for the neighbor's cousin's kids because there's nothing else to do. Or that I walk past my elementary school teachers at the mall and they look away, embarrassed at all my untapped fucking potential.

TYLER. Dean.

DEAN. These burgers need more marinade.

> *(*DEAN *is already up the steps and into the house.* TYLER *picks up the tongs he dropped on the ground and flips the burgers. Pause.)*

TYLER. Do you want a burger or a brat?

CHARLOTTE. Surprise me.

TYLER. You're still so smart, Charlotte Finn.

CHARLOTTE. Vintage sweaters and the right fountain pen, my friend.

TYLER. But you still have no clue.

CHARLOTTE. Please enlighten me.

TYLER. See, you never came around to hang out with us in these woods when we were in school. You always had other places to be.

CHARLOTTE. I studied.

TYLER. Well my buddy Dean studied too. He wanted to get out just like you did, as much as you. And you know what? He still had time for the people that mattered to him. He still has loyalty to those folks. He cares about us.

CHARLOTTE. Of course he does.

TYLER. We were out here every weekend. Every summer. You were nowhere to be found, Charlotte Finn. So how the hell do you know who he is or what he's about? Where were you?

CHARLOTTE. I know how great you think he is.

TYLER. We didn't have anything, just change to keep a quarter of gas in the tank, we were our own good times.

CHARLOTTE. I guess I missed them.

NAN. Well I didn't, and they were fun.

CHARLOTTE. Should my feelings be hurt?

NAN. Tyler, what are you saying?

TYLER. So why do you show up now that we actually have some stuff that might matter? Families, backyards, futures. Don't you have a nifty life out in Portland?

CHARLOTTE. Sure. It's different out there.

TYLER. Cleaner air, better jobs, smarter people –

CHARLOTTE. You're smart, Tyler.

TYLER. I'm not talking about me. Did I say me?

NAN. No.

TYLER. Shush.

NAN. Well who are you talking about?

TYLER. Just. People. In general. Out there. Aren't they better people, like you say?

CHARLOTTE. Portland is better for me because it's not here. For me. I didn't say anything about other people.

NAN. Stop it, Tyler.

TYLER. So all your plans worked out, Charlotte. Congratulations. That guy doesn't need the reminder.

CHARLOTTE. We're old friends saying hello.

TYLER. Hi. You can go home now.

CHARLOTTE. *(To* NAN.*)* Well, aren't you curious about me?

NAN. Huh?

CHARLOTTE. You were a freshman. Didn't you hear all about me?

NAN. Weren't you valedictorian or something?

CHARLOTTE. Salutatorian. No speech.

TYLER. Thank freakin God almighty.

CHARLOTTE. C'mon, didn't you wonder how I found time to be so smart and be such a slut?

NAN. Um, I'm not sure I heard that –

CHARLOTTE. And why wouldn't you, right, because whatever some dudes say, it has to be the truth, right?

NAN. Maybe. You didn't deny what happened. You smiled.

CHARLOTTE. So if it were you –

NAN. You wore lipstick.

CHARLOTTE. So?

NAN. Bright red. You played the part.

CHARLOTTE. Dean was the only guy who'd level with me. He told me what they were saying. He had the guts. He's my only friend.

NAN. So you want him back, is that it?

TYLER. She didn't have him.

CHARLOTTE. A crush is so simple.

NAN. You're in her backyard, Charlotte Finn.

CHARLOTTE. Who?

NAN. Jess. You've gotta do right by Jess.

CHARLOTTE. Look, this place is really cute. But I've known these guys longer than either you or this Jessica –

NAN. Well I've been counting down to this party for two weeks now, and I'm going to shake my can and have some fun.

CHARLOTTE. It's a big night for you.

TYLER. It's just a barbeque, jeez.

NAN. Right. So you had better just sit in a lawn chair and tell us funny stories about Portland with your legs crossed.

CHARLOTTE. Excuse me –

TYLER. Dean. Get out here.

CHARLOTTE. Jessica is the one who invited me, his girlfriend.

NAN. If this is going to be weird –

TYLER. Right now, Dean.

CHARLOTTE. Dean saved me.

> *(A moment.)*

Smart girls are invisible. But he singled me out, he saw what I couldn't. He knew you weren't going anywhere, Tyler. So he chose me instead. And when it almost derailed and I was too mortified to leave the house or tell my parents, Dean stood by me. He pushed me to study even harder, get the scores, find the right college. I owe him.

> *(Turns to **TYLER**.)*

The one time I try to be like you and your posse of meatheads, it blows up in my face. I should never have followed you out to the woods.

NAN. So what did happen out here, huh?

TYLER. Kids' stuff, babe.

NAN. Why not? It's not like anybody's around much anymore. Tell us.

> (DEAN *enters from the house with a covered dish, using potholders.*)

DEAN. Green bean casserole coming through.

NAN. Yum.

> (DEAN *sets it down on the picnic table, tearing off the tin foil.*)

TYLER. I'm gonna need a Pepto Bismol as a chaser if we're eating that.

CHARLOTTE. Well I'm starving.

DEAN. Jess is so excited you came early, Charlotte. She's got this big grin on her face.

CHARLOTTE. She's a really pretty waitress, Dean.

DEAN. It's a sign you're here.

CHARLOTTE. You think so?

DEAN. Maybe you'll start to rub off on me.

CHARLOTTE. We should talk.

DEAN. You're right, I do feel content.

TYLER. Dean, buddy –

DEAN. But this town can tell us the truth about ourselves. It can't help itself, it crackles. Maybe it's time to listen.

CHARLOTTE. Maybe.

> (*A car honks out front, followed by another.* TYLER *grabs his whiskey and pulls* DEAN *with him as he checks.*)

TYLER. Aw, it's Mike and Caitlin.

DEAN. You girls okay?

NAN. Uh.

CHARLOTTE. We're fine.

> (DEAN *hugs* CHARLOTTE, *surprising her.* NAN *watches, not quite knowing what do or where to go.*)

DEAN. You're right. This is kind of crazy.

CHARLOTTE. Sorry.

DEAN. I mean, you chose to come back here –?

CHARLOTTE. Where else would I go?

> (**DEAN** *goes around the side of the house to greet the arriving guests.*)

DEAN. Move the car over there, asshole.

> (**CHARLOTTE** *starts to follow him, but* **TYLER** *blocks her, clipping the air in front of her with the tongs from the grill.*)

TYLER. Careful.

> (*Lights dim.*)

End of Act One

ACT TWO

Scene One

(Night. The party is winding down. Soft music plays from the trailer. **CHARLOTTE** *and* **JESSICA** *sit at the picnic table, laughing and drinking together.* **DEAN** *is collecting garbage and hauling away a trash can full of bags. There might be beer bottles in the cluttered fence that he has to grab.)*

CHARLOTTE. It took a while to feel comfortable.

JESSICA. New places take time.

CHARLOTTE. And guys there were no help.

JESSICA. Oh we speak the same language.

CHARLOTTE. Touchy-feely men with five degrees, all wearing the same fleece vest.

JESSICA. Fixer-uppers.

CHARLOTTE. Eventually, you have to surrender to the natives and start composting, or the whole place will drive you nuts.

JESSICA. You're a pioneer, Charlotte. Forging out over the Rocky Mountains and across the desert to Portland on your own.

CHARLOTTE. Well, I flew there.

JESSICA. Most stop in Chicago.

CHARLOTTE. Weren't you in Chicago, Dean?

DEAN. Yeah, the Reader and the Sun-Times both wooed me that way. Right out of college.

CHARLOTTE. Were you writing the horoscope?

DEAN. No, crime beat on the South side. Drug dealers blown to bits by rookie cops who break down sobbing when I tried to get a quote.

CHARLOTTE. That's impressive.

DEAN. Great town. I miss it.

JESSICA. I lived in Cleveland for a while when I was in my twenties, you know, just to be closer to where the action was. We were driving up to visit guys in the Flats every weekend anyway –

CHARLOTTE. Oh the Flats.

JESSICA. But actually living there was skuzzy and grunge bands would raid the grocery stores on their way out of town after gigs. I could never find tortillas. And then it all sort of stopped. Clubs closed. I dated a promoter who OD-ed and moved to a ranch. I missed the heyday up there by like six weeks.

CHARLOTTE. You need home sometimes.

JESSICA. And when I got back, everybody was pairing off and getting married, or already married and trying to have kids.

CHARLOTTE. Those aren't the only options.

JESSICA. Married gals tell me that. So I saved up and bought the first available lot in this neighborhood.

CHARLOTTE. We're both pioneers.

JESSICA. This was my wedding and my first kid.

CHARLOTTE. It's a nice house. This part of town was so dark and foreboding when we were kids. I thought someone was always watching us from the trees.

DEAN. Who?

CHARLOTTE. Now it is Tom Sawyer fences and sprinkler systems. Crazy.

JESSICA. It's still pretty desolate on the next street over, but city planners are trying to step it up, knock down the abandoned buildings, so we're making our own little patch of it the best we can.

DEAN. Yes, I know we need to fix up that fence.

JESSICA. Dean's quite handy.

CHARLOTTE. Surprise.

DEAN. She bought me a tool belt I refuse to wear.

JESSICA. Yeah, if I had known that about him I would have said yes the first time he asked me out. Dean, you haven't stopped moving all night.

DEAN. *(Knots a bag of trash.)* You make me work for it.

JESSICA. Sit down with us.

DEAN. I got a list of my own, babe.

CHARLOTTE. You make lists now too, Dean?

JESSICA. It's a game we play.

DEAN. Sometimes I even win.

JESSICA. I let you win. Was he always this cute?

CHARLOTTE. He's lost some of his edge, but yeah.

DEAN. My edge?

CHARLOTTE. Some. C'mon, you talked about your ten year plan and how you wanted to nab exclusives with international dictators. Bylines and deadlines and passports and – your upper lip would get all sweaty when you talked, you were possessed. You're softer now.

DEAN. Maybe.

JESSICA. He interviewed me when I bought this house, you know, for the Tribune.

CHARLOTTE. *(Turns to DEAN.)* You wrote for the paper here?

JESSICA. He was very tough.

CHARLOTTE. You were, huh?

DEAN. Election year, city council seats, a corruption trial. There were stories to tell that year.

CHARLOTTE. So that's how they lured you back.

JESSICA. And he came to meet me with his hair parted, dressed to the nines in a shirt and tie. A little hat, like a comic book.

DEAN. I was setting an example for my staff.

CHARLOTTE. Your staff? What happened to national correspondent, Dean?

DEAN. You tell me. Haven't seen you on TV handing it back to Diane Sawyer.

(Pause.)

CHARLOTTE. Ouch.

DEAN. Well, who's got your byline these days, Finn?

CHARLOTTE. I didn't realize I was supposed to bring my CV with me.

DEAN. We've got Wi-Fi inside.

CHARLOTTE. Why don't you finally sit still and I'll tell you.

(JESSICA rises.)

JESSICA. Dean, I'll take that down the driveway.

DEAN. Um, it's heavy, there's a broken bottle –

JESSICA. *(Takes the trashcan from him.)* I got it.

DEAN. Did my friends scare you off?

JESSICA. They're very funny.

DEAN. Tyler must seem demure compared to Mike and Caitlin. They were quite smitten with the place, the food. You.

JESSICA. We need more fun.

(To CHARLOTTE.)

It was really nice having you here.

CHARLOTTE. Are you saying goodnight?

JESSICA. Yup.

CHARLOTTE. Well I'm glad you ran after us in the parking lot.

JESSICA. Your mom always leaves her To-Go bags on the table.

CHARLOTTE. She lives on your Cobb Salad.

JESSICA. Dean seems to get his mojo back when you're around.

DEAN. I'm standing right here.

JESSICA. I mean it. I haven't heard you talk about Chicago or your byline in months. Old friends trigger that stuff for each other, I guess. And if chasing one of them down is what you need, that's what I'll do. Night.

> (*JESSICA snaps the elastic on* **DEAN**'s *underwear and exits around the side of the house with the trashcan.*)

> (*The music has stopped in the trailer.*)

NAN. (*Off, giggling.*) You scum bucket.

CHARLOTTE. Nan has a ton of energy.

DEAN. She's young. And she has to keep up with Tyler.

CHARLOTTE. I can't believe he's a dad.

DEAN. Not touchy-feely enough for you?

CHARLOTTE. It looks like a good life.

DEAN. I'm unemployable, my best friend lives in the backyard –

CHARLOTTE. How is that possible? You went to college.

DEAN. There are no jobs. It's a flat tire version of where we grew up, despite these new developments they keep sinking money into. Nothing opens, nobody hires.

CHARLOTTE. But you stay chipper.

DEAN. I romanticized this place. Older folks give up.

CHARLOTTE. My parents have.

DEAN. Now it's pulling me under.

> (*Pause.*)

We make choices and some of them work out, some don't. We still have to take responsibility for the whole mess.

CHARLOTTE. I could use you out in Portland.

DEAN. Ha.

CHARLOTTE. I mean it.

DEAN. Yeah, I'm yearning to be an artisan radish farmer.

CHARLOTTE. The way you move around and pour the drinks, laugh at receding hairline jokes and rub people's shoulders. You're not afraid to be intimate. They would lap you up in Portland. You could lead us, Dean.

DEAN. It's my party, my night.

CHARLOTTE. You know their kids' names.

DEAN. I still like these people. We get each other.

CHARLOTTE. And you don't look down on them.

DEAN. Being fired humbles a person.

CHARLOTTE. How did they fire you? You own the wardrobe. I don't get it.

DEAN. Two papers, one budget. And I was so into it. I know the history of this town and all it's had to weather over the past fifty years, my grandfather was a foreman so I got the true stories, and – I don't know –

CHARLOTTE. You can tell me.

DEAN. Writing its future seemed like a good opportunity.

CHARLOTTE. Of course.

DEAN. But they give you the title without the manpower to stay on top of every little detail, so –

CHARLOTTE. I wish you had called me.

DEAN. Yeah, I could have used your mirth.

      (**CHARLOTTE** *laughs*.)

See, I miss using my vocabulary. Everything's "shit fuck" and "you know what I mean?", but nobody's actually saying anything.

CHARLOTTE. She doesn't talk that way.

DEAN. *(Re:* **JESSICA**.) Diploma, no degree.

CHARLOTTE. She seems to do fine without one.

DEAN. How many did you wind up with?

CHARLOTTE. Um.

DEAN. C'mon, brag a little.

CHARLOTTE. Three. Little good they do me out there. I work at a comic book store and I sell little yarn dolls on the weekends at the flea market down by the river. And my house has a slanted front porch nobody's going to fix for me, and a whole wall of used books I never open. We sit around a lot in Portland.

DEAN. Really?

CHARLOTTE. We're both going under.

DEAN. Why don't you move? Isn't that what we're supposed to do when we get dissatisfied, rent a U-Haul?

CHARLOTTE. Would you come with me?

(Pause.)

My life, this life right now, is derailed. And the only time I felt any sense of possibility or future is when I was with you, Dean.

DEAN. It's easy to feel that way. But Tyler won't let me. He's a numbskull sometimes, but he never gives up.

CHARLOTTE. I never told them who it was, the guy that night in the woods. The one who stayed behind with me after the tailgate party. I wouldn't say his name.

DEAN. You were cross-eyed drunk that night.

CHARLOTTE. I was trying to be different.

DEAN. It would have been worse for you if you had said –

CHARLOTTE. Said what? His name?

DEAN. You knew what they'd say, how they'd see you after that. I agreed with you.

CHARLOTTE. Were you ashamed of what we did?

DEAN. What are you talking about?

CHARLOTTE. I'm not going to say it out loud, with your girlfriend in earshot.

DEAN. Look, I know it wasn't the most honorable moment in our lives, but we were all teenagers. I see them skateboarding in the streets now, and I wonder if I was ever that age –

CHARLOTTE. Okay, now you're fucking with me.

DEAN. – but I remember how eager we were to twist stories to make ourselves look better and others look bad. I was looking out for you. You have to know that, at least.

CHARLOTTE. I know that after all this time, you should own up to what you did –

DEAN. What I did?

CHARLOTTE. You invited me to come. You wrote out directions to get to the clearing in the woods, where the party was going to be. Nobody else was going to invite me. I kept my head down on the desk for three years, and then you asked me –

DEAN. You were sweet and funny. I wanted them to notice you.

CHARLOTTE. You held my hand.

DEAN. I pulled you over to say hello to everyone.

CHARLOTTE. Music played from the stereo in the car with the cracked headlights on. I brought two bottles of vodka from the back of my parents' cupboard. And I relaxed and made jokes, and they laughed. Everybody chased each other with sparklers through the trees –

DEAN. It was our last summer together. We were so ready to start our lives.

CHARLOTTE. You noticed the shirt I was wearing, my bra straps poking out. My cup was full, always full, so I kept drinking and cut loose. You showed me where to put my hands.

DEAN. That didn't happen with me.

CHARLOTTE. Don't try to put this in some sentimental little box, Dean. It won't work. I won't let you. It was – it is – too important. You were sweet. You wiped my chin with your bandana when I threw up, then you still kept kissing me.

DEAN. I didn't kiss you.

CHARLOTTE. Everybody else was gone. Acorns digging into my thighs and pinesap sticking to my nipples when you turned me over on my stomach. So gentle. I cried into the leaves that night, out of relief. I was being seen.

DEAN. I went home. Track practice at 6am.

CHARLOTTE. It was you.

DEAN. Tyler had a cracked headlight that he never fixed. He wore bandanas.

CHARLOTTE. Don't try to wiggle out of this, Dean.

DEAN. I tried to drive you home, but you insisted –

CHARLOTTE. You flipped me over so I could straddle you, so I could control it. I felt like me, finally. And in the light of day, I'm the smart girl with the dirty knees. Is that why my life didn't work out?

DEAN. Your life is fine, Charlotte.

CHARLOTTE. I want to be exceptional, not fine.

DEAN. And you think I don't? Have you been obsessing about that night for twelve years? That's crazy.

CHARLOTTE. If I could go back to that sloppy desperate girl, I would slap her across the face. I would tell her what's waiting for her, the years of living in studio apartments and constantly switching my email address so people would think I moved to Europe.

DEAN. We still have options.

CHARLOTTE. Do I have you?

DEAN. You're not hearing me. You were all over Tyler. He got drunk and you had sex. He couldn't keep his big mouth shut. I admired you so much.

CHARLOTTE. Why?

DEAN. I was your friend.

CHARLOTTE. We have to get out of here. It's dying.

DEAN. It wasn't me. It was Tyler.

CHARLOTTE. Details don't matter. I miss dreaming.

    (Rises.)

I think we killed the whiskey.

DEAN. That bottle's pretty drained.

CHARLOTTE. *(Tries to kiss him.)* Hold still.

DEAN. What are you doing?

CHARLOTTE. I can't – you stand straighter.

DEAN. Charlotte? I'll call your husband.

CHARLOTTE. Him.

DEAN. He's at your house?

CHARLOTTE. He makes me feel like an ottoman when we're alone.

DEAN. Are you okay to drive?

CHARLOTTE. You're making me leave?

DEAN. No, but – we can't stay out here all night. We have to go back.

CHARLOTTE. Drive with me to Portland.

DEAN. I care about our future.

CHARLOTTE. She's so lovely. But she wants you to stay here and sprinkle fertilizer. I look at you and I see the overachiever applying for his passport so he can jump on a plane at a moment's notice for an assignment in Burma. Every time you got a job or turned in a story, didn't you think of me? Didn't you wonder when we'd run into each other again? Didn't you hope to?

DEAN. You're married.

CHARLOTTE. He'll nap in the backseat.

DEAN. I'm not going to lie and say I haven't wondered about you. And I can't see myself crossing off lists for the next twenty years. You were supposed to have the answers, Charlotte Finn, and bring them back to me.

(**CHARLOTTE** *pulls her passport out of her pocket.*)

CHARLOTTE. Mine's renewed as of last week. Let's fill up these pages.

DEAN. Is this why you came here?

CHARLOTTE. Maybe. Where's yours?

DEAN. In a drawer. Upstairs.

CHARLOTTE. Did you let it expire?

DEAN. Of course not.

CHARLOTTE. *(A moment.)* We are inevitable, Dean.

DEAN. I like being a nice guy. It's harder than being a selfish jerk.

CHARLOTTE. Nice guys get the girl.

DEAN. Part of being the nice guy is taking hits for the team. And Jess and me are trying to figure out how to be a team. I say this without irony or rancor or –

CHARLOTTE. Good.

DEAN. Or embarrassment. I love Jess.

CHARLOTTE. But does she need you?

DEAN. She does.

CHARLOTTE. Or are you the hot guy who relies on her for everything –

DEAN. That's not who we are.

CHARLOTTE. Are you sure about that?

DEAN. You were here a couple of hours. You don't know us.

CHARLOTTE. While you were off getting marshmallows for the s'mores, Tyler told me that Jess pays all the bills and leaves the Help Wanted section of the paper for you to find –

DEAN. Don't.

CHARLOTTE. Well I needed you to stick up for me when everyone was talking about what an easy slut I turned out to be. I just smiled and there were no consequences for anybody. So you owe me, Dean.

DEAN. It's been real illuminating seeing you again. But I think I am going to make you leave now.

CHARLOTTE. Have you ever driven across the desert at night?

DEAN. Of course not.

CHARLOTTE. It changes you.

DEAN. Maybe I don't want to change. You're trying to twist the past because you wanted to show everybody, get revenge. If it makes you feel better, I'm buying groceries from the homecoming queen.

CHARLOTTE. She's still here?

DEAN. This is where I'm supposed to be.

CHARLOTTE. You're scared. I'm leaving town tomorrow. I hope you're with me.

(**TYLER** *appears in the doorway to the trailer, wearing boxer shorts and flip-flops.*)

TYLER. Reunion time?

CHARLOTTE. I have to go.

DEAN. Yes you do.

CHARLOTTE. We can make this anything we want it to be, Dean.

DEAN. Thanks for the donuts.

(**CHARLOTTE** *exits along the side of the house.*)

What else did you tell her?

TYLER. Oh here we go –

DEAN. What the hell, Tyler? Did you catch her crazy when you did her against that tree?

TYLER. Hey.

DEAN. Or can't you help yourself?

TYLER. What are you talking about?

DEAN. Look, I'm always doing you favors that you never say thank you for, but please, if you are going to blab all my problems to near-strangers, then I won't be helping you or your clan out anymore.

TYLER. I was making conversation.

DEAN. She wants me to run away.

TYLER. Told you she was screwed up.

DEAN. And the whole time, she thinks I'm you. That I was the one who strutted down the halls and said whatever about her –

TYLER. Listen to me. Nobody here is that person anymore. So drop it.

DEAN. You wish it were that easy.

TYLER. Your freakin life is not my fault or my problem. Neither is that nutcase's. I don't make messes I can't clean up.

(*A moment.*)

You wanna run away again? Go right ahead.

(**TYLER** *goes back inside, slamming the door.* **DEAN** *throws his beer bottle against the fence, watching the clutter shift around it.*)

(**JESSICA** *appears in the doorway to the house.*)

JESSICA. Dean? Turn those lanterns off –

DEAN. Will you stop telling me what to do?

(*Pause.*)

It's like we invite the trash to come hang out. Why don't people throw their shit away?

JESSICA. Come up to bed.

DEAN. Why did you invite her here?

JESSICA. What's wrong with you?

DEAN. You have no idea what kind of history she has with Tyler. Then he weasels out of any responsibility so I have to fix it? She's completely delusional.

JESSICA. I was being nice.

DEAN. You were testing me, to see if I could handle having her sit here with her marriage and her success and her life.

JESSICA. Maybe.

DEAN. Well she's just as lost as I am, Jess. It really blew up in your face.

JESSICA. You're still figuring it out.

DEAN. Not fast enough, apparently. Get out the damn newspaper, let's find me a brand new spanking job tonight.

JESSICA. I thought she'd spark something in you.

DEAN. Sure, if you orchestrate it.

JESSICA. I'm trying to help. Your resume file just sits there on the desktop of the computer.

DEAN. Is that why I have your panties on? So you can feel ownership of me?

JESSICA. I thought you wanted to be close.

DEAN. So I'd feel even less of a fucking man –?

JESSICA. Don't swear at me.

DEAN. Did you tell my friends? Did you brag about it?

JESSICA. No, it was between us, a secret –

DEAN. You got drunk enough tonight.

JESSICA. I'm not drunk.

DEAN. Just so you'd have something to talk to them about, what you tricked me into doing.

JESSICA. Trick you? You wanted to put them on. Why are you freaking out on me? What did she say?

DEAN. No, you know what? You know what?

> *(Pulls off his shirt, takes off his pants.)*

Is this what you want to see?

JESSICA. What did that woman say to you?

DEAN. Is this what you want them to see? How you mastered me? Is this it?

> *(Stands naked in* **JESSICA***'s underwear.)*

Is this your man, Jessica?

JESSICA. Good night, Dean.

> *(***JESSICA*** *slams the door as she goes back inside.*
> **DEAN** *starts up the stairs, but stops when the light inside the house goes out.)*

> *(***DEAN*** *crawls over to the pool, dunking his head.)*

> *(In the trailer, we hear* **NAN** *softly moaning.)*

TYLER. *(Off, insistent.)* Let me inside you. C'mon. Let me inside you.

End of Scene

Scene Two

(Next morning. A lawn mower is out in the yard.)

(JESSICA is smoking a cigarette, sitting on the steps to the house. She is still in her bathrobe.)

(NAN enters from the side of the house, carrying a bag of groceries and a large box of diapers.)

NAN. Ooh, diaper sale Monday's not pretty. Some woman got her finger smashed grabbing for the last thing of wipes.

(Stops when she sees JESSICA.)

Did Tyler forget?

JESSICA. Forget what?

NAN. His freakin route. I leave a post-it on his penis so he'll remember when he wakes up.

(JESSICA throws down her stack of mail.)

JESSICA. He did his route.

NAN. Mom agreed to keep the girls until this afternoon. We got stuff to do.

JESSICA. Call him.

NAN. Last night was real great, Jess.

JESSICA. You think so, huh?

NAN. Your food rocked.

JESSICA. That marinade's all anybody talked about.

NAN. Yeah, Tyler only makes it for occasions.

JESSICA. Just a silly drunken night.

NAN. But Dean begged him, so –

JESSICA. Why did Dean have to beg?

NAN. Tyler's allergic to chili peppers. He breaks out.

JESSICA. So why does he – that doesn't make sense.

NAN. The sauce was your secret weapon.

(Pause.)

JESSICA. I'm glad you were here, Nan.

NAN. My family thought I was crazy when I went with Tyler, threatening to drain my gas tank so I wouldn't drive over to the west side and see him. But I couldn't help myself. He takes care of me.

JESSICA. That's real sweet.

NAN. Dean knows how to take care of you.

JESSICA. Your buddy Dean's leaving.

NAN. What?

JESSICA. I don't know where he went or – we had a fight, and – now he's not here.

> (*Takes a long drag.*)

Can you get Tyler for me? Please?

NAN. If you got your mail, he'll circle back.

> (*JESSICA stands.*)

JESSICA. Okay, which way does he go?

NAN. We can't chase after him on his route.

JESSICA. Dean's gone.

NAN. His supervisor checks up on him, he could get into trouble –

JESSICA. That's not my problem. He knows what happened, Dean would have told him's all I'm saying –

NAN. No, Jess. We'll get him fired and we need that job.

JESSICA. Then what good are you right now, Nan? Huh?

NAN. I'll stay with you. Dean wouldn't break this up. He loves you.

> (*JESSICA laughs at her.*)

He does. Stop laughing.

JESSICA. He got bored. C'mon Nan. Grow up. I know I've got this small house and my job and this little life, but it's something. Why would he give up all this just to get rid of the Me part that comes with it?

NAN. Dean snapped when he got laid off. You were here.

JESSICA. His drawers are empty upstairs and there are files missing on the computer.

NAN. What did you fight about?

JESSICA. It's stupid. He said I was bossy.

NAN. You are in charge.

JESSICA. Some nag is not what I want to be. He just sits here feeling sorry for himself.

NAN. He does stuff you don't see, Jess.

(A moment.)

JESSICA. I made him wear my underwear last night.

NAN. Ooh.

JESSICA. We weren't, you know, *connecting* very much and then all of a sudden he was up there, ripping them off –

NAN. Yeah?

JESSICA. And shoving them in his mouth while we –

NAN. Dean? Go on.

JESSICA. So I thought – I got him to put them on. I was being sexy and up for anything and – I can always hear the two of you down here huffing away.

NAN. I'm just picturing Tyler's little cheeks sticking out of my thong.

JESSICA. Anyway now he's gone.

NAN. Tyler will know where he is. We'll find Dean.

JESSICA. You sound so sure.

NAN. I know how you feel about us.

JESSICA. No –

NAN. And I'd like to be the gal who saves her nickels to buy the big house, or listened to my parents and went away to college, but I wanted other things. All of us being together like this makes me happy. I hope I'm your friend, Jess.

(Picks up her bags.)

Now let's stash this stuff and find your man.

JESSICA. He's not my –

NAN. If you don't say it, nobody else will. Own it.

> *(A moment.)*

JESSICA. Let me help.

> *(JESSICA picks up the diapers and follows NAN over to the trailer.)*

NAN. Dean's too smart for his own good. I don't think you've ever been inside my home before.

JESSICA. No, I guess not.

NAN. Wait until you see what this puppy can do.

> *(JESSICA follows NAN into the trailer with the groceries.)*
>
> *(We hear an electric siren – a loud version of the "Superman" theme – coming from the speaker of the trailer.)*
>
> *(TYLER runs in, wearing his mailman's uniform and carrying his empty mail sack.)*

TYLER. What happened? What's wrong?

JESSICA. *(Out.)* Where is he?

TYLER. Why the freak did she use the baby alarm? Her mom's still got 'em hostage.

JESSICA. Where did he go?

TYLER. Dean?

NAN. *(Back out.)* Did you bring my Good and Plentys?

TYLER. Why did you use the alarm? I'm not gonna get that noise outta my head.

NAN. We need to find Dean.

TYLER. Party went late last night. Maybe he slept in for a change.

JESSICA. He's not upstairs.

TYLER. Well I haven't seen him. What's going on?

NAN. He's missing.

TYLER. No, he's not. His car's still here, the keys – did you look for his keys?

JESSICA. They're on the table, that doesn't mean anything.

NAN. Dean likes to walk.

TYLER. Maybe he went on a fuel run –

JESSICA. Knock it off.

NAN. Tyler.

TYLER. We throw this big party, and you park the lawn mower out front at the crack of dawn? Real subtle, lady.

JESSICA. I'm mowing the lawn. Nobody else will do anything around here unless I beg them –

TYLER. Now hold on –

NAN. She doesn't know where he is, babe. She's scared.

TYLER. *(Calls.)* Dean.

JESSICA. Did he say anything to you at all?

TYLER. He wouldn't dare – Dean.

NAN. Where's your cell?

> (**NAN** *holds out her hand as* **TYLER** *fumbles around.*)

TYLER. He's not going to cross the street without telling it to me.

JESSICA. So find him.

> (**TYLER** *hands over the phone.* **NAN** *presses buttons.*)

NAN. *(A text.)* "Time to go."

JESSICA. I knew it.

TYLER. That could be from a week ago –

NAN. 7AM. This morning.

JESSICA. What did he tell you about Charlotte Finn?

TYLER. Charlotte Finn?

NAN. Tell her.

JESSICA. He went off with her, that's where he is.

TYLER. Why would he go off with Charlotte Finn?

JESSICA. Last night, while sitting here, I had this feeling – I tried to ignore it, drink it away, but I woke up –

TYLER. Charlotte Finn didn't fuck him in high school, I'm quite sure she's not going to fuck him now.

NAN. Who said anything about fucking?

TYLER. *(A moment.) Freaking.* Sorry –

NAN. We have to help her. What did he mean, "Time to go"?

TYLER. Stop pestering me about it, Nan.

JESSICA. *(With the phone.)* Where do I find the texts?

TYLER. It's an older model. You should have no problem.

JESSICA. Fuck you.

NAN. Tyler, did he talk to you about the underwear?

TYLER. Wait, you think because we're stuck on your property that I'm going to have some sort of allegiance to you over my best friend? Doesn't work that way, *ma'am.*

JESSICA. Well, I'm sick of the bibs and the diaper wipes and the pool and the apples and all this junk. It just keeps coming and I don't –

    (Kicks the fence in the back.)

If Dean's gone for good, there's really no point is there? I'm sorry, Nan. I can't do this anymore. If you don't find him, pack up your brood and go.

NAN. Jess, wait –

TYLER. We've got plans already in motion, lady. Who needs this? You'll all be alone in your precious centimeter of suburbia. Good luck.

    (Turns to NAN.)

Underwear? What the hell does that mean?

NAN. Tyler get back here.

TYLER. Dean has the right idea, trying to get away from this lunatic.

JESSICA. Maybe he's finally trying to break away from *you.*

TYLER. I really doubt it. I'm his only family left.

JESSICA. You limit him. He won't apply for honest-to-God real jobs here because he's afraid he'll end up like you.

TYLER. Dean knows how to leave town if he wants to. I can handle it if he does it again. Can you?

NAN. Call him.

JESSICA. What?

NAN. Why don't we just call his phone? He'll think its Tyler and pick up. We'll nab him through a subterfuge.

TYLER. No don't use me like that.

NAN. Do it, Jess.

JESSICA. I'm not – I don't know –

NAN. C'mon let's stop fighting and actually do something.

TYLER. She's scared to find out, that's why.

WALT. Hello there.

> (*All turn.* WALT *is standing there, having come around the side of the house. He radiates Portland.*)

JESSICA. What are you doing?

WALT. Spelunking.

TYLER. Who the hell are you?

WALT. I'm Walt. Hello.

TYLER. You can't just come strolling back here –

WALT. It's a great little street. She told me this was all trees once. I see they cut them down to make that field next door. I found this branch, thought I'd make it into a walking stick. I hope that's okay. I whittle.

NAN. Sir, did you have a stroke?

WALT. And I've also got to ask you about the mailbox.

JESSICA. My mailbox?

WALT. It's shaped like a factory I saw once that makes chocolate.

JESSICA. We're from Hershey.

WALT. Pennsylvania?

JESSICA. You know it.

WALT. Remarkable. Could I buy one, maybe, same as yours?

JESSICA. My granddad made it.

WALT. Wicked.

TYLER. Can I help you with something, guy?

WALT. Perhaps. I seem to need a finger in the right direction.

JESSICA. Are you lost?

WALT. Not emotionally. This town feels so familiar to me, like the back of my hand really, even though it's my maiden voyage here. But we pulled off the turnpike, I just felt like I was reuniting with a comfortable old friend. Or a coat I used to wear.

JESSICA. Were you here for the party?

WALT. The party?

TYLER. He wasn't.

WALT. He's right. My invitation was extended and then evaporated.

TYLER. Who are you?

NAN. Give him a dollar, Tyler.

WALT. Excuse me, I assumed this was the kind of street where I could swing by and have a glass of ice tea with real sugar. I'd give up one of my nipples for some real sugar. Maybe watch a parade celebrating an assassinated president roll by. You know?

TYLER. It's not 1955, guy.

NAN. We're a nice place.

WALT. You are? I'm unconvinced so far.

JESSICA. What do you want?

WALT. I thought she might have come back here. Taken refuge.

TYLER. Who?

WALT. Maybe she felt safe back here. I do.

JESSICA. Do I know you?

WALT. We shook hands in a parking lot yesterday. You don't remember? Par for my course.

JESSICA. Who are you?

WALT. Walt. I belong to Charlotte.

(A moment.)

NAN. Are you sure about that?

WALT. We're married. Do you know where she went?

JESSICA. She's gone too?

WALT. Has someone else disappeared? Uh oh.

TYLER. No one's going anywhere, we just – *misplaced* –

WALT. See, I stayed home and played Balderdash with the in-laws like a good sport. Nice people, but resentful of each other at this stage. Stressful game, so I went on to bed. We're sleeping in her room, which still reeks of her adolescent CK One. She tumbles in late, drunk and snorting. Thanks for that.

TYLER. Hey, she brought the whiskey.

WALT. Charlotte's allergic to alcohol. It makes her unpredictable. I never touch it.

NAN. Maybe you should.

JESSICA. So she was with you?

WALT. Not so fast. I woke up and she was gone. Her mother found this address and sent me here. She always leaves a skein of yarn when she goes, but not this time.

JESSICA. Oh no.

WALT. Annoying little hobbies like knitting become the world to you when your better half has vanished.

TYLER. Jessica. Dean did not run off with Charlotte Finn.

WALT. Dean?

TYLER. It just couldn't happen, he wouldn't – he doesn't have the guts.

JESSICA. Do you know Dean?

WALT. Charlotte can talk. And last night, as she was landing on her face, all she babbled about was Dean's fingers on her arm and the way his lips moved. Maybe I'm here to meet him?

NAN. He's not here either.

(JESSICA races up the stairs and into the house.)

TYLER. Get in there, Nan.

NAN. What am I supposed to say? This doesn't look good.

TYLER. Babe, go.

NAN. Wait, Jess. Don't freak. Dean's a douche bag.

>   (NAN *exits.*)

TYLER. Dean didn't go anywhere. He's – out job hunting, he's – he doesn't do this.

>   (**WALT** *is running his hand through the water in the pool.*)

WALT. Whirlpool in the suburbs.

>   (*Pulls out a black marker and rolls up his sleeve, and writes it down.*)

Amateur poet.

TYLER. He didn't go with her.

WALT. Charlotte's sentimental. She wouldn't like it if we started fighting over something she's done. She has a big heart.

TYLER. You're wasting time here.

WALT. I think we all are. When I first got to know Charlotte, she always had one eye over her shoulder, like she was waiting for someone to creep up from behind and trap her. They're long gone.

TYLER. Dean doesn't creep.

WALT. Are you Tyler, then?

TYLER. Yeah. I'm his best friend. I know what he can do and what he won't do, and this isn't –

WALT. Sure it is.

TYLER. Dean's not after your wife.

WALT. Yeah, you got there first. Didn't you have sex with my wife against an oak tree?

TYLER. She told you that?

WALT. You didn't wipe her chin with a bandana because she was too full of vodka to pull her skirt down herself?

I told you. Charlotte can talk. And she keeps that night alive.

TYLER. Look, she grabbed at me.

WALT. Of course she did.

TYLER. She didn't leave me alone. We were seventeen.

WALT. We're capable of a lot when we feel trapped. Charlotte was backed into a corner, and this Dean showed her how to work her way out. No wonder they grabbed hold of each other again.

TYLER. *(Re:* JESSICA.*)* He wouldn't do that to her.

WALT. I offer very particular qualities to her. We have a good life in together in Portland. Slower pace. She's terrified of being ordinary. And every so often, she has to prove to herself that she hasn't peaked as a human being, and that the future's not going to be a waste. Off she goes. And as long as she's happy and the only person she's hurting is me, what's wrong with that? Right? She knows I can take it.

TYLER. Dean was just her friend.

WALT. Well that's a relief.

TYLER. And you can't fix her –

WALT. Peeling her off the floor isn't a fix. It's love. So much Charlotte Charlotte Charlotte. She blurs details and makes up stories that fit her own idea of herself. She thinks he's you.

TYLER. He likes feeling needed.

WALT. And she *needs*. They're a perfect match.

TYLER. I didn't plan it or anything, she just felt so untouchable. Then she came after me. The mysterious Charlotte Finn, you know?

WALT. It's her weapon.

TYLER. And they had plans. Off to school, leaving town. All of a sudden there's this chance to be part of it.

WALT. So what's this Dean doing back here?

TYLER. He's an optimist. Same as me.

(**TYLER** *pulls a wet beer from the cooler.*)

WALT. People drink an awful lot here.

TYLER. Beer clears my head. You want one?

WALT. I'm good. I guess you can drink in Milwaukee or Detroit just as good as here. Does it give you courage, does it whisper sweet nothings in your ear?

TYLER. Sometimes.

WALT. It practically serenades Charlotte.

TYLER. Dean didn't run off with some girl from high school. That's all she is to us now, some girl.

WALT. That's all she is to *you*. Charlotte stepped on my foot in a club in Portland, and my world stopped. I knew she would bring me nothing but frustrated joy. I didn't care. It's the way she arches her eyebrow, gets me every time. Dean is doomed and maybe he needs to realize that for himself.

TYLER. Dean's doing fine here, he's building his life back up –

WALT. You need to let go.

TYLER. I can't.

WALT. We're all a stop along the way for each other. For such a tough-looking guy, you are weak, Tyler. You're not Dean. And screwing my wife didn't make you her, either. You're you. And if you follow everyone else around, if you invest in their lives to the point you're ignoring your own, you'll have to start over, again and again. Work your way across the country, through towns like this one. Fresh starts every time, and then problems, your "issues", start seeping in again. Then you're out west, on the precipice, with nowhere left to go. I have to make due. Charlotte's my life raft. I have nothing to do but wait for her to come back down to earth.

(*Kicks off his shoes.*)

Mind if I dip my feet in?

TYLER. You're just gonna wait?

WALT. He's your friend. Find them.

TYLER. I'm not good with messes.

WALT. Obviously. This pool's full of leaves.

(Scoops some out and steps in.)

Ah. Real nice.

TYLER. You're welcome.

WALT. If it makes you feel better, she's still chasing the wrong guy.

TYLER. Look, my girl Nan's pregnant again –

WALT. Clever girl.

TYLER. – So I'm not interested.

WALT. I was referring to myself.

(Peers down into the water.)

There's something pink down on the bottom.

TYLER. What?

*(**WALT** fishes out the underwear **DEAN** was wearing in the last scene.)*

WALT. How kinky.

(Tosses them on the ground.)

Men playing boys. Well, Tyler. It's been nice breaking the ice. But you had better hope they surface soon. Otherwise, I'm calling the police here and reporting my car stolen, that your friend in all his rage and frustration over getting laid off from his big important job, a really public embarrassment –

TYLER. How did you know about that?

WALT. My wife knew. She's known for a while now. And so he kidnapped her and took off in my car. He's crazy right now, like most of America. It's a pretty good story for a police report.

TYLER. Dean didn't do anything wrong.

WALT. Well, someone's got to take responsibility. And women tend to look at us differently when we betray them. She's a tough cookie, that girl there. I know that look. I've been married four times.

(A moment.)

But let's give them some time to sort it all out, shall we? This sure is a nice way to kill an afternoon. Wow.

(**WALT** *closes his eyes, feet in the pool.*)

End of Scene

Scene Three

*(Later, late afternoon. Lawn mower is gone. Lawn
furniture has been stacked by the side of the house.)*

*(**DEAN** is pulling the trash and debris from the
fence onto the ground. He is disheveled, wearing a
torn and ripped suit. He continues working, faster,
and pulls the tie from around his neck. He looks
for a bag and starts collecting the trash into it.)*

*(**TYLER** runs on from the side of the house.)*

TYLER. Dean. What are you doing?

DEAN. *(Continues to work.)* We scatter crap like this all the
time out here. Beer. Paper plates. We buried pot out
here in Ziploc bags. All I want to do is clean it up, get it
done. What's wrong with me?

TYLER. You left a fucking mess, Dean.

DEAN. *Freaking.*

TYLER. No, with Nan I say "freaking", with you it's back to
fucking –

DEAN. No, you make a big speech about swearing in front
of your kids, we're going to do what you fucking say,
right? Isn't that the way you want it?

TYLER. What's going on?

DEAN. Just shut up. Shut. Up. She hates this fence, you
know? I need to buy new paint, replace the broken
slats. She deserves it.

TYLER. Where did you go?

DEAN. And I deserve to have a home with her. I'll earn this
if I have to –

TYLER. Her husband was here. He wouldn't leave. Dean –

DEAN. Don't.

TYLER. Where did you go?

DEAN. Charlotte was waiting for me, perched on the hood
of her car. My collar's crisp. My passport's in my back
pocket. We're ready to go.

TYLER. That's not who you are anymore.

DEAN. Don't you think I know that? We're in the car and she's moving the entire time, kicking off her shoes under the gas pedal, fitz-ing with the radio stations. And she won't stop talking about the co-op in Portland and the fantasy book club she's in. And I realize as we barrel towards the Interstate, deciding whether to head East or West, that she's not going to be enough. Even this girl, who believed so hard in me when I couldn't, she won't be what I want. What do I want, Tyler?

TYLER. What's wrong with your leg?

DEAN. Then she starts about that night, that fucking night, and how we could recreate that night over and over again. How did she give you that kind of power?

TYLER. What did she do to your leg?

DEAN. I told her to slow down, she wasn't even stopping to breath, and we're going so fast the car's rattling. We're near the Interstate, and I open the door and throw myself out –

TYLER. You jumped?

DEAN. I landed in some bushes.

TYLER. Man, you're bleeding.

DEAN. She yanked the car to the side of the freeway and came after me –

TYLER. Charlotte chased you?

DEAN. Screaming "Should I tell people now? Should I tell them all now?" Why did you tell people, you asshole? I left her with you and she pawed at you and you acted like it was a sports event. And I helped you. I let you get away with it. You and me deserve each other.

(**DEAN** *goes back to pulling debris out of the fence.*)

TYLER. Let me see your leg.

DEAN. I can fix this.

TYLER. C'mon, I think you really hurt yourself.

DEAN. Go back to folding baby socks.

TYLER. Hey I'm happy as a clam folding baby socks –

DEAN. I never saw you the same way again. You made it easy to leave here. I'm your friend out of habit.

TYLER. Well I picked you. And I picked Nan. You think I didn't have choices too, buddy? Just because I didn't have the standardized test scores doesn't mean I didn't choose.

DEAN. The fact you got the family's a joke.

TYLER. You're my family, Dean. We can be enough for you. This can be enough. Charlotte –

> *(**CHARLOTTE** has appeared alongside the house, also very disheveled, her feet are bare.)*

CHARLOTTE. We made love.

DEAN. It wasn't me.

CHARLOTTE. But I can still feel you.

DEAN. You have it wrong. You were with Tyler.

CHARLOTTE. We were supposed to take on the world. Coffee on a red-eye. Photos on the wall with ambassadors. You said we could do all that, and I believed you. I hoped because of you, Dean. And when I laid back under that tree, and I could see the night sky stretching out, this town didn't look so small. We began here, we're not supposed to end –

TYLER. You asked me to hold you. You were cold so I gave you my letter jacket. I bought it myself, it was my favorite thing in the world. You asked to see my tattoo.

CHARLOTTE. I wanted to like bad boys –

TYLER. So I pulled open my shirt so you could see my back –

CHARLOTTE. I traced my fingers along the black lines –

TYLER. It's blue.

CHARLOTTE. Blue.

TYLER. And it was new, so it still sort of hurt –

CHARLOTTE. You winced.

TYLER. You giggled and called me tough guy –

CHARLOTTE. I pulled on your chest hair. Oh God.

TYLER. Then you stuck your feet in my hiking boots and raced me back to the truck. We were so drunk.

CHARLOTTE. Oh God.

TYLER. I drove you home and kissed you good night. Good guys drive you home and kiss you good night –

CHARLOTTE. And you wiped my face with your bandana. You took care of me. It was you.

TYLER. Yes. You were special, Charlotte.

CHARLOTTE. I was?

TYLER. You are.

DEAN. Yes, you are.

CHARLOTTE. I'm so tired.

      (A moment.)

You can still come with me, Dean. He belongs here –

DEAN. Stop chasing me, please.

CHARLOTTE. But aren't we supposed to be winning? Didn't you go with me because you still want to believe – ?

DEAN. Story's not over, Charlotte. And I'm not that kid anymore. It's easier to hope.

      (To **TYLER**.*)*

Right, buddy?

CHARLOTTE. So if you had stuck your fingers up inside of me and stared down at me with the look of awe this asshole had plastered on his face, do you really think you'd still be taking out the garbage?

DEAN. Who knows? But this is where I am now. Where are you?

      *(***WALT*** is standing alongside the house, watching.*
      NAN *is beside him.)*

CHARLOTTE. Then you're an idiot if you think there's a future in this nothing town, this crater of mediocrity –

WALT. Enough, Charlotte.

CHARLOTTE. *(Turns.)* What did I tell you?

WALT. You've said enough.

CHARLOTTE. Do I have to write it on my face so you'll understand the message? I'm not going with you anymore.

WALT. I found your shoes.

> *(Holds them out.)*

Your parents want to take us to dinner before we head out. Figure we have time to get you a shower.

CHARLOTTE. God, you followed me?

WALT. I drove the car. It's parked in the driveway. I talked the police out of impounding it.

CHARLOTTE. You just think of everything, don't you?

WALT. What else was I supposed to do, Charlotte? Every man has a lady. And you're mine. Now let's go.

CHARLOTTE. I don't want to go back to Portland with you.

WALT. And why's that?

CHARLOTTE. I'm bigger than Portland, I'm – I have my passport!

WALT. Maybe we can go somewhere else then.

CHARLOTTE. No. You're not understanding me –

WALT. I understand you just fine, sweetheart.

CHARLOTTE. Stop. Don't do this in front of them. Don't try – to – love me.

WALT. But I do.

CHARLOTTE. I don't – want – to believe you –

WALT. Shh. We can just go home if you'd like. We'll make some new plans of our own. You are beautiful and I deserve some beauty in my life. You deserve someone like me, Charlotte. We'll go forward together, like we should. How does that sound?

CHARLOTTE. You're nuts, Walter.

WALT. How does that sound?

CHARLOTTE. I'll try.

WALT. You are a very brave woman, Charlotte Finn. You'll do more than try.

> *(Turns to others.)*

Ohio has been such a treat.

CHARLOTTE. I still believe in us, Dean.

DEAN. We're just getting started.

> **(WALT** *and* **CHARLOTTE** *are gone.* **NAN** *comes up to* **DEAN**, *slaps him across the face.)*

TYLER. Hey.

NAN. I don't know what's worse, watching your girlfriend fall apart down to her cuticles in there, or knowing we have forty-five minutes before we have to rescue our girls. We stick together, Dean. Don't forget it.

DEAN. I won't.

TYLER. You don't have to resort to violence, babe.

NAN. Inside. I made you a list.

> *(***NAN*** exits in the trailer.)*

TYLER. Well I better get cracking then –

> *(A moment.)*

I wanted to think she picked me, Dean. And then I'd be part of your future.

DEAN. You are the future.

TYLER. Nah, my kids are.

> **(TYLER** *follows* **NAN** *into the trailer, closes the door.* **DEAN** *ties the bag of trash, starts filling another one.)*

> **(JESSICA** *appears from inside the house.)*

DEAN. Look what I found.

> **(DEAN** *reaches for the panties on the ground.)*

JESSICA. Throw those away. I don't know what I was thinking.

DEAN. Why aren't you at work?

JESSICA. I called off.

DEAN. You did? You?

JESSICA. I was too upset to drive.

(**DEAN** *tosses them into the trash.*)

What have you been doing?

DEAN. We talk about fixing up this fence, cleaning it out. I thought it was time to actually do it.

JESSICA. Is that why you came back?

DEAN. Look, Jess –

JESSICA. I know I can be a little bit much, that I'm controlling and bossy.

DEAN. Strong.

JESSICA. And it pushes men – well, you – it drives them away. And I'm very aware of that about myself, but it's really too late to re-boot my personality, okay?

DEAN. I like who you are.

JESSICA. And I don't know what she promised you, or what kind of life you think you can have by following her, but the problems you have, Dean – even if it's just the inability to pick up the damn newspaper – are all going to still be there, no matter where you are. You can't flee every time it gets hard. And I love those problems because they come with you. Okay?

DEAN. Okay.

JESSICA. And I'm not saying this because I'm fending off a bunch of men my own age hanging around looking lonely, I just – I like you a whole lot.

DEAN. Well I love you.

JESSICA. *(A moment.)* What do we do now?

(*Indeed, we can see the sky and green grass that was hidden by the debris. It casts more light into the yard that wasn't there before.*)

DEAN. Maybe it's time to grow that garden we talked about.

JESSICA. When?

DEAN. Well I talked about it.

JESSICA. No, when do you want to start digging?

DEAN. Well, I – I just need to get some – today?

JESSICA. Ready when you are, Dean.

DEAN. *(Takes her hand.)* Come here.

JESSICA. Where are we going?

        (DEAN kicks off his shoes, pulls off his shirt.)

  We both won't fit in there.

DEAN. If we stick together real tight –

JESSICA. Should I pull out the floating toys? Some goggles?

DEAN. No room for all that. Just us.

JESSICA. Why would I do that?

DEAN. Because I asked you. C'mon.

      (DEAN holds out his hand.)

      (JESSICA looks at her cleared fence, her sun-drenched yard, her house, and then kicks off her shoes and steps into the pool with DEAN.)

      (Blackout.)

End of Play